THE INQUIRING LADY

Drusilla had to admit that Arabella Fletcher was the most beautiful belle in all the realm. But the questions Arabella put to Drusilla were quite plain inde

"What do you think o... Arabella asked.

"I find him a man too... having his own way about things," Drusilla answered.

"Do you find him handsome?" Arabella persisted.

"He might be if he smiled," Drusilla said. "But one has the feeling he almost never does."

"In short, you dislike him?" Arabella asked eagerly.

"You need not fear me as a rival, if that is what you have come here to find out," Drusilla said.

Arabella smiled. "Even had you professed a tenderness toward the poor fellow, I should have been reassured. Someone told me you were pretty. And so I suppose you are in a rather unremarkable way. But scarcely a threat to *me*."

That, however, remained to be seen. . . .

The Nabob's Widow

[For a list of other Signet Regency Romances by April Kihlstrom, please turn the page. . . .]

The Nabob's Widow

by

April Kihlstrom

A SIGNET BOOK

NEW AMERICAN LIBRARY

SIGNET, SIGNET CLASSIC, MENTOR, PLUME, MERIDIAN and NAL BOOKS
are published by New American Library
1633 Broadway, New York, New York 10019

Ⓢ SIGNET TRADEMARK REG. U.S.PAT.OFF. AND FOREIGN COUNTRIES
REGISTERED TRADEMARK-MARCA REGISTRADA
HECHO EN CHICAGO, U.S.A.

First Printing, July, 1986

1   2   3   4   5   6   7   8   9

PRINTED IN THE UNITED STATES OF AMERICA

1

The woman who stood on the front lawn of Lawford Manor, near the village of Cropthorne, wore a dark-blue cloak of the finest wool, full gray boots of soft kid leather, and a hat that not the most inexperienced observer could have mistaken for other than expensive. Neatly curled locks of fair hair escaped from that hat, and fine blue eyes stared out over the sloping countryside. Her cloak concealed her figure but nothing could conceal her height, which was a little above the usual. Had she smiled, she would have seemed beautiful. It was a blustery winter's day, however, and one might have been pardoned for wondering if that was the reason she looked so grim.

And yet Drusilla Lawford cared very little that she shivered with the cold. If the past year had not been sufficient to acclimate her to British winters, neither had it been sufficient to destroy the delight of seeing snow again after six years spent in India. Nor was it the view that distressed her. Lawford Manor was one of the neatest country houses about, and while Drusilla could not deny that it was a far cry from what she had expected, she was most unlikely to complain.

Indeed, Drusilla Lawford had not known what to expect. Hugo had had so little time to tell her anything before he died, and she had returned to England knowing only that he had promised to provide for her. She had known—everyone had known, of course—that Hugo Lawford had made a fortune in India and had returned to England to enjoy that fortune. But when he came back out to India, Hugo had lost no time in telling everyone that most of his estate would be tied up for a nephew. And so it would stay. He had no notion of becoming a matrimonial prize merely because a number of ambitious mothers thought it would be delightful for their daughters to marry such a wealthy nabob.

Yet he had married Drusilla. Married her over her own protests and promised to provide for her, as well, out of the funds and such that were not entailed. And then he had died and Drusilla had returned to England because those were Hugo's wishes and because there was nothing to keep her in India anymore.

"Just a small country house," that's what he had told her on his deathbed. "A small country house I'm sending you back to," he had said. "I hope you won't be disappointed."

Small! The word scarcely began to describe the charming Georgian structure behind her with its twenty rooms furnished with all the favorite pieces of a man who had spent most of his life in India; it rested on three hundred acres of land and boasted a small stable, as well as a pond and folly. To Drusilla, the youngest daughter of an impoverished clergyman, it seemed a veritable palace.

In India, it was true, she had grown accustomed to being waited upon by servants and being treated with deference by the natives, but that was not the same thing as in England. Drusilla had never been foolish enough to suppose that she would move in the first social circles back home as she had in India. It just was not the same thing.

Then, tilting her chin up, Drusilla asked herself, Why should I not move in the first circles? Mama was judged to have thrown herself away on a younger son, but both families are most respectable. If it were not for my silly pride, Mama's aunt might have introduced me to London society. Now that Drusilla had married so well, Aunt Matilda had suddenly discovered an interest in her affairs, and never mind that she had ceased to speak to her niece, Drusilla's mother, these past thirty years or more. Drusilla lowered her head again. It was more than pride, of course, that had kept her from going to London. She was not only in widow's weeds, but her mother and father had died of the same cholera outbreak that had killed Hugo Lawford.

Fortunately Drusilla Lawford had no further time for such reflections, for at that moment a young figure hurtled into view, checking only at the sight of her. The boy's eyes widened in astonishment as he blurted out, "Who are you?"

Amusement and exasperation warred for a moment but Drusilla had had three brothers of her own and she was not unaccustomed to such cavalier treatment. The boy who confronted her reminded Drusilla most of Johnny. He had the same large brown eyes beneath an unruly shock of brown hair, and his clothes, while far more expensive, were just as rumpled as Johnny's had ever been and as covered with snow as his had been covered with dust. The major difference was that this boy was healthy, as

Johnny had not been. But it was the sameness that led Drusilla to try to tease him. "I am the lady of the manor," she said in her grandest voice.

The boy was not deceived. His eyes unabashedly raked over Drusilla, noting her above-moderate height, blond curls, and large blue eyes. That her clothes were of the latest fashion mattered not in the least to him. "No, you're not," he said accusingly. "There isn't any lady of the manor. Hugo never married, you know. Besides, ladies of manors don't have laughing eyes."

"They don't?" Drusilla asked, intrigued at this notion.

"No," the boy said emphatically. "And I've met enough of them to know. So who are you?"

"Well," she answered thoughtfully, "suppose you call me Drusilla? And tell me your name. I haven't seen you about before."

"That's because my father and I have just returned from the Americas. Business," the boy replied loftily.

"I see. Well, you still haven't told me your name," Drusilla persisted.

"Oh. Right. It's Alfred. Alfred Pensley. But everyone calls me Freddie," the boy replied.

"How do you do, Freddie?" she said brightly.

The boy was intelligent, however, and had not missed the constraint in her manner. "Is anything wrong, ma'am?" he asked, hesitating.

"No, of course not," she said hastily. "It is just that I received a note from your father today. I presume he is your father? Lord Pensley? He means to call. Some . . . some business, you see."

"My father?" Alfred asked with a frown. "Pity it's business."

In spite of herself Drusilla laughed. "Why do you say that?" she asked.

"Because I like you," the boy said darkly. "And I don't like Mrs. Fletcher. Mrs. Rumstead, our house-keeper, says Mrs. Fletcher wants to marry m'father, and I shouldn't like that at all."

"Does your father wish to marry her?" Drusilla asked.

"He don't wish to marry anyone," Freddie replied frankly. "But I expect it would be better if he did. He's been very lonely since Mama died. But Mrs. Rumstead says he don't even know Mrs. Fletcher wants to marry him. I hope she won't."

"Why not?" Drusilla asked reasonably. "Isn't she pretty? I've heard she is, and very kind as well."

Alfred kicked up the snow with his boot. "That's what everyone says," he agreed reluctantly. "But she hasn't got laughing eyes. And I don't think she likes boys. She told me I was horrid once. That was before we went to America."

"Did she? Why?"

"Because I gave her a frog." As Drusilla burst into peals of laughter, he added earnestly, "I meant it as a present. Truly I did!"

"I'm sure of that," Drusilla answered as gravely as she was able. "Unfortunately most ladies wouldn't see it as such."

"But you'd understand, wouldn't you?" he asked shrewdly.

Drusilla paused, "Yes, yes, I suppose I would. But then, I had three brothers and lived in India, so I'm not quite like the ladies you've met."

"India!" Alfred said with delight. "Will you tell me all about it? Hugo used to tell the most wonderful stories. Did you live there long? Did you see elephants? Tigers? Why ever did you leave there?"

Again Drusilla laughed. "Why don't you come inside and have some cakes and tea?" she said. "Unless you would prefer hot chocolate. It's a frightfully cold day."

"Tea," Freddie said decisively. "That's what grown-ups drink."

"Very well, tea it shall be," Drusilla said, hiding her smile, "and I shall tell you all about India. In return, however, you must tell me about yourself."

"There isn't anything to tell," Alfred said with a sigh. "I haven't had any adventures. Except going to America, and that isn't nearly as exciting as India."

"I'm not so sure about that, but in any event I don't want to hear about adventures," Drusilla said reasonably. "I want to hear about you. And what sorts of things you like. Is it a bargain?"

With a shrug that clearly expressed his bemusement, Freddie nodded, and together the two mounted the steps at the front of Lawford Manor. "Ought we to go in this door?" he asked doubtfully.

"What? Do you still think me a liar?" she rallied him. "I assure you it's all right; I really do live here. I married Hugo about a year ago, just before he died. We met in India."

"Did you love him?" Freddie asked. Drusilla flushed, and he went on, "I ask because my father says Hugo deserved to have someone love him. He was the greatest fellow, you know, and I should like to think he was happy just before he died."

Recalling Hugo Lawford's last days, the delirium and the pain, Drusilla could not bring herself to tell the boy the truth. "Hugo was a wonderful fellow," she agreed quietly, "and I promise you I did what I could to make his last days comfortable ones. I only wish I could have done more."

Freddie turned his large brown eyes toward her. "Then that's good enough," he said with certainty. "Hugo always told me that that's what mattered . . . doing the best you can, I mean."

For a moment tears filled Drusilla's eyes. "Thank you," she said. "I think I see why Hugo liked you so much, Freddie."

The smile that lit the boy's face prompted a matching one from Drusilla, and it was at that moment that Witton emerged from a room off the entryway and saw them. As he later told Cook, it was the first time he had seen a smile on Mrs. Lawford's face since she came to live with them, and a very nice sight it had been, too. Most correctly trained, however, he merely bowed to Drusilla and said as he took her winter cloak, "Company, madam? The Pensley boy, I believe."

She smiled warmly down at Freddie. "Yes, I understand he was a great friend of Mr. Lawford's. We should like tea, for the two of us, in the drawing room." She paused and asked the boy, "You don't mind that, do you? The drawing room, I mean."

Freddie shook his head, pulling off his own wet jacket. "It's not like other drawing rooms," he said wisely. "It's far more interesting. Hugo used to take me there, as well, to show me things."

"Good, that's settled, then. Tea in the drawing room, Witton."

"Very good, madam," he said with another bow. "You'll find quite a nice fire going there."

Drusilla turned back to Freddie and took him down the hall. "Now, tell me about yourself," she said with a smile.

Sometime later, a tall, erect figure paused on the front steps of Hugo Lawford's house to survey the same scene Drusilla had been contemplating such a short time before. From the contemptuous curl of his lips and the frowning aspect of his very handsome face, it might be inferred that the gentleman was not pleased with what he saw. Or perhaps it was the lady he had come to call upon that displeased the fellow, for one look at the riding coat and breeches revealed beneath his overcoat would have sufficed to inform the observer that he was not dressed in his Sunday best. Nor did he appear to have made any effort to tame the unruly locks of brown hair upon his head. Though that solecism may have been due to the sort of reckless gallop the gentleman was well-known for. In any event, the gentleman did not wait long before he mounted the rest of the steps and slammed the knocker sharply upon the door.

It was opened almost immediately. "Lord Pensley!" Witton said in a tone of intense gratification. "How good to see you again."

"Thank you, Witton," his lordship replied with a smile. "How are you? And Mrs. Witton?"

"Very well, m'lord, and fancy you remembering to ask. You'll be wishing to see Mrs. Lawford, I expect."

The smile disappeared from Lord Pensley's face. "Yes, I shall," he said curtly. "Quite a facer, that must have been. A new mistress and no warning to you and Hugo himself gone for good."

Witton's own face was now precisely correct as he replied, "It is not for me to speculate upon such matters, m'lord. But may I say that Mrs. Lawford has been a delight to us all. Your coat, m'lord?"

Without a word Pensley handed Witton his beaver hat and overcoat with its fashionable layers of capes.

As he followed Witton toward the drawing room, however, Pensley could not help sneering to himself, So she's won over the servants already, has she? Clever woman.

The drawing-room doors were flung open and Richard Pensley felt a sharp wrench at the knowledge that this time it would *not* be Hugo who greeted him. Instead, it was a young woman. At least, he noted irrelevantly, she has the decency to wear black.

Drusilla, meanwhile, took stock of the man who had come to call. There was nothing to fault in his figure, however casual his attire might be. Her caller seemed every inch the gentleman, and after a moment she spoke. "Lord Pensley? You must be looking for your son. He just went home."

Startled, Pensley replied, "My son? Freddie?"

"Yes," she said, a puzzled expression upon her face, "he was here, but he just left. Isn't that why you came?"

Meeting her eyes, Pensley said, "No, that isn't why I came. I had no notion, in fact, that my son has been making a nuisance of himself by coming over here. We haven't been home long enough for that, I should have thought. I shall speak to him directly I return home, however, and make sure you are not disturbed again."

Alarmed, Drusilla Lawford held out a hand in protest. "No, don't do that. Please," she said. "Freddie is a charming boy and I quite enjoyed his company."

"Charming boy?" Pensley asked doubtfully. "I think so, of course, but I am well aware the ladies are inclined to think he runs a trifle wild."

"Surely no more so than a boy ought to at his age,"

Mrs. Lawford said. "Why I remember Johnny was just such a child before . . ."

She stopped and Pensley prodded, "Before what?"

The color left Drusilla's face. "Before he died. A good many years ago, I'm afraid. He always had been a sickly child." She paused then made an effort to smile. "That, however, is none of your concern. May I ask why you did come to call, if it was not about Freddie?"

Pensley hesitated. "Shall we be seated?" he asked. When they were, he went on, "I've come on business. I did send 'round a note, this morning. Didn't you receive it?"

"Yes, yes, I did," Drusilla replied evenly. "You did not state, however, when you meant to call, and I had not thought it would be so soon. Nevertheless, you are welcome. Business, you said?"

"I am calling as trustee of your late husband's estate. You did know I was the chief trustee, did you not?" Pensley asked with a frown.

The young woman looked down at her hands. "Yes, yes, I suppose I did. It's just that I was rather distressed when Mr. Nicholson explained things to me, and I had almost forgotten. Is there . . . is there a problem with the estate?" she asked, raising her eyes to meet his again.

Richard Pensley leaned back in his chair, trying to make up his mind about Drusilla Lawford. She was younger than he had expected and with a grace that he had not thought to find. Obviously she was not quite the callous jade he had first envisioned when he had learned of the marriage. On the other hand, perhaps she was merely a very accomplished actress. Certainly she was not some beauty that Hugo had fallen in love with in his dotage. Attractive, yes; a beauty, no. It did not occur to Pensley that Drusilla Lawford was one of those women whom black does not suit, causing her to appear sallow in the room's winter light.

In turn, Drusilla stared at him. Another woman would have been affronted by Lord Pensley's careless attire. Drusilla was not. Instead, she noted the wariness in his expression and wondered why he had come.

Gentlemen of the *ton* had been known to ask how he managed the intricate folds of his neckcloth, and others might have envied the plentifulness of his curling dark hair. Pensley's answer had always been a carelessly waved hand and the comment that he was fortunate in his choice of valets. Drusilla found herself thinking that it was not his manservant who accounted for the neatly turned leg or broad shoulders that no doubt left many feminine hearts in danger of breaking. He had entered the room with an assurance Drusilla envied. No valet had taught him that or accounted for the height that topped her own by more than a head. Nor for the eyes that now seemed deep with anger.

And Pensley *was* angry. When he had first heard of Hugo's marriage and Nicholson had told him the details of the will, he had even felt rage. For he had always liked and admired Hugo Lawford and knew he deserved better than to be leg-shackled to someone who could have cared nothing more for the man than a desire for his wealth.

"A problem with the estate?" he said, at last, aloud. "No, the problem lies rather with you, I'm afraid."

"Me?" Drusilla asked, startled. "Whatever can you mean?"

Pensley looked at his hostess. Again Mrs. Lawford felt the eyes spark with anger and then dim in sadness. Without haste his lordship answered, "Hugo Lawford was not a misogynist. He liked women. But one of the things he said to me the last time we talked was that he positively never, in his life, intended to marry."

2

Her eyes wide, Drusilla Lawford stared at Lord Pensley for several long moments. At last she stood and turned her back on him as she paced the length of the room, a fine Indian carpet beneath her feet. "I see," she said quietly. "That was, I gather, the opinion Hugo expressed to everyone?"

Pensley nodded, and she went on, in a conversational tone, one hand resting on a brass elephant Hugo had brought home years before, "That explains, of course, why no one has come to call on me. I did rather wonder, you know. Hugo's family was quite respectable even if he did go out to try his hand at trade in India. And he never said anything to make me believe he was unpopular here. But then, of course, we had so little time together that there was so much he had no chance to tell me."

"A rushed marriage, was it?" Pensley asked coolly.

Drusilla met his eyes levelly. "You know very well it was," she said bluntly. "It was also, however, very much what Hugo wanted. Whatever you may believe, I did my best to discourage Hugo from taking such an extreme step. But there was no stopping him. You might say he married me out of pity."

"You could have refused," Pensley pointed out reasonably.

Once more Drusilla turned her back on him. So softly that he could scarcely hear, she said, "I would it had been so simple." More loudly Mrs. Lawford added, "There is obviously no point in trying to convince you I did not marry Hugo for his money. So I wish you will merely state your business and leave."

For a long moment Pensley did not answer. With her tears held in check only by the greatest effort, Drusilla could not bring herself to turn around and see why not. When Lord Pensley's voice came, it was from right behind her shoulder. "I wanted to see for myself the woman Hugo had married."

"And now that you have?" Drusilla asked with a lightness she did not feel.

"And now that I have, I shall reserve my judgment," he replied seriously, not troubling to match her tone. "You are not the predatory harpy I expected. But believe that Hugo married you out of pity, I cannot. He was not a fool. Had he wanted to provide for you, there were other ways."

"Perhaps he wished to pay back his nephew for some offense, real or imagined, by disinheriting him of some of the wealth he expected," Drusilla pointed out quietly.

"Perhaps," Pensley agreed, "but again, there were other ways to do it. No, for some reason I cannot begin to fathom, Hugo must have admired you. It is beyond belief that Hugo would have married you if he did not."

Drusilla was scarcely aware of the sigh of relief that escaped her. Once more she was able to turn and face him. "Would you care to stay and take tea with me, then? Although I fear it may be cold by now," she added, indicating the tray that held the remains of her tea with Freddie. "I promise I shan't try to trap you in my net as you believed I may have done with Hugo."

"I think I should very much like to stay," Pensley astonished her by saying. "I've never minded cold tea, and we have," he reminded her, "my son to discuss."

Drusilla smiled, aware of a tumult in her breast and grateful at kindness she had not looked for in this man. "Good. But I shan't really subject you to cold tea. Mrs. Witton would never forgive me if I did," she said in some confusion.

Drusilla reached for the bellpull, but there was no need, for at that moment a maid rapped on the door of the drawing room, then entered with a new tray of hot tea and pastries. In spite of herself she laughed. "Tell Mrs. Witton she is the most excellent housekeeper I have ever seen," Drusilla told the girl, who curtsied as she removed the old tea tray.

Lord Pensley smiled as well. When they were seated again, he said, "Tell me, Mrs. Lawford, what did you really think of my son's manners?"

Drusilla smiled. "I found him a most refreshing child. And one I liked very much."

"You sound as if you mean that," Pensley said with no little surprise.

"And why not?" Drusilla demanded as she poured them each a cup of tea.

"Because he has run far too wild since his mother died four years ago," Pensley replied bluntly. "Nor did my trip to America help. Freddie was everywhere spoiled and pampered, and I was too busy with business to stop it. Not that I should have known how even if I wasn't."

"It must have been very difficult for Freddie losing his mother," Drusilla said thoughtfully. "He could have been no more than six. How did it happen?"

"He was five," Pensley said curtly. "My wife died trying to give birth to our second child. The baby didn't live long either. Freddie was away, staying with a cousin, when it happened, and he has refused to be separated from me ever since. Which is how I came to take him to America when I went. I had to make final arrangements about my wife's estate there. It had been part of her dowry. And I could not bring myself to leave Freddie behind, though my sister would have been delighted to have him."

Once more Drusilla was thoughtful. "He seems a happy child," she said at last, "and not one subject to horrible fears."

"Freddie is not," Pensley assured her, "save on the subject of being away from me for more than a day or two."

"You have done a great deal for him," Drusilla said quietly. "It would not have been surprising to find him withdrawn or afraid."

It was then that Drusilla saw one of Pensley's rare smiles. A moment, however, and it was gone. "I shan't bore you with my problems," he said curtly. "Tell me about yourself."

"Me?" She looked at him with some surprise. "You cannot wish to hear my dreary history."

"Oh, but I do," he assured her, the cynicism once more evident in his voice.

"Very well, I was born Drusilla Crandall. My father had a small parish up north and my mother bore him six children. Johnny and I were the youngest, almost afterthoughts, one might say. My two sisters died at birth, Johnny only after we reached India. My two surviving brothers, you see, had each gone out, in turn, to serve in the East India

Company, in hopes of making their fortunes. They never did, but they are still there, doing modestly well, both married to very nice girls.

"Eight years ago my father decided we should all go out to India. Partly to visit Keith and Peter, and partly to serve as a missionary. That was before the new charter, of course, so Papa couldn't say that was what he wanted to do. He simply got himself attached as a sort of clerk to Hugo's staff. That was how I first saw him. Not that Hugo ever noticed me, then. I was still a child and he was about to return to England. I didn't see Hugo again until about a year ago. There was trouble brewing and he was to invest-igate, but he died of cholera before he had much of a chance to do so. My mother and father died about the same time. Two weeks before, in fact. Hugo was kind and offered to marry me. Insisted, really, and in the end I agreed. It was his idea that I should come back and take up residence here. I still can't quite believe it, you know."

"And your brothers? Do you miss them?" Lord Pensley asked gently.

Drusilla laughed. "My dear sir, do you realize how immense India is?" she demanded. "I saw my brothers perhaps twice in the entire time we lived in India. And as they were more than ten years older than I was, they have never had a great deal of time for me. No, if there is anything I miss it is India itself. And yet I cannot help but feel that it is not our country and that we will never be entirely at ease there."

"We?" Pensley asked with raised eyebrows.

Drusilla smiled. "The British," she explained. "Our customs are not theirs, nor are they ever entirely likely to be. And we, we understand so little about them that I cannot help but think . . ." She paused and shook her head. "No, you will think I am foolish."

"Go on," he prodded gently.

She took a breath. "Very well. I think that we shall do very well, for a while. The East India Company, I mean. Gaining land and rents and trade and that sort of thing. But in the end the sheer differentness will defeat us and it will be their country again. Does that make any kind of sense to you?"

Pensley smiled at her. "It is very much the kind of thing Hugo used to tell me. In strictest confidence, of course. It's not the sort of view an officer of the Company is supposed to go about espousing. It wouldn't make him very popular, you know."

"I do know it," Drusilla agreed with a wry smile. "And yet Hugo and I loved India no less because of it."

"My dear Mrs. Lawford," Pensley said in mock horrified accents, "one is not supposed to *love* India, one is not supposed to try to civilize it!"

Together they laughed, then Pensley rose to his feet. "I must go now, Mrs. Lawford," he said. "There are some matters that will need your attention concerning Hugo's estate, but that can wait until another day. In the meantime, if I can be of assistance, please let me know."

Drusilla held out her hand and he took it. "Thank you," she said. "You have been very kind."

"Kind?" He looked at her sharply. "I didn't mean to be. I merely wanted to see what you were like and satisfy my curiosity."

A surge of anger rose in Drusilla's breast. "And have you?" she asked evenly.

He raised his eyebrows and regarded her coolly. "In part," he conceded.

"Oh? Well, pray tell me if there are any other questions you would like to ask," Drusilla retorted icily.

"Only one, for now," he replied maddeningly.

"And what is that?"

"How old are you?"

"I've just turned twenty, though I cannot conceive of what importance that may be," Drusilla answered.

Pensley bowed. "I thought so, but I needed to be sure. Mrs. Lawford, it is important. Didn't you realize? Under the terms of Hugo's will you and your inheritance are my responsibility until you come of age. And that will not be, under the terms of his will, for another five years."

Startled, Drusilla said, "Are you sure?" He nodded. "You mean you have charge of what funds I may have?"

"More than that," he told her. "It is a trifle irregular, but I even have right of approval over whom you may marry . . . if you wish to remarry before the five years are out."

"Impossible!" she said. "How can you?"

"Well," he agreed apologetically, "I do not precisely have right of refusal. I do, however, have the power to cut you off without a penny if I do not approve of your choice of husband. It is, I am afraid, quite legal, however irregular it may appear to be. Nor can I say I am any more pleased than you are at Hugo's last wishes."

Slowly Drusilla sank back into her chair. "Well, this is a facer," she said at last.

"Why?" Pensley demanded, regarding her sharply.

"Was there someone you intended to marry? Even so, recollect that Hugo's will does not forbid you to remarry before you turn twenty-five, it merely says that you must have my approval if you wish to keep Hugo's legacy to you."

"It is, I suppose, a considerable one?" Drusilla asked. Pensley inclined his head and she went on, "Who stands to inherit if I forfeit by marriage. Do you?"

"No," Pensley told her curtly. "I have no idea where it goes. That, it appears, is Nicholson's concern. I only know that neither you nor I will have it, in that event. I ask you again: are you contemplating marriage?"

Drusilla turned her large blue eyes up at him. "No," she said quietly, "I am not. I am simply stunned that Hugo chose such a provision, though I suppose I should not be surprised. There is no reason he should not have written his will in any manner he chose."

"How generous of you," Pensley said ironically. "Nevertheless, as you have said, it is a facer. And with that thought, I shall leave you. I have an urgent appointment elsewhere and I am afraid I shall be late as it is."

Once more Drusilla rose. "I shan't thank you for coming to call upon me," she said frankly, "for you have made it very clear that was meant as no kindness."

He nodded. "I shall, however, thank you for taking my scapegrace son in to tea. Will you mind if he comes calling again? If you do, I shall speak to him, but he has always loved this house."

Drusilla shook her head decisively. "I should not mind in the least," she said.

"Thank you. And good day, Mrs. Lawford."

"Good day, Lord Pensley," Drusilla replied, her back ramrod-straight.

It was perhaps fortunate for her pride that Pensley could not know how soon after he left the drawing room Drusilla fled upstairs to the privacy of her room, crying one more time. She cried not so much for how she had been misunderstood in her marriage to Hugo but out of homesickness for a time when the question could not have arisen. Even after a year she missed her family very much.

3

Lord Pensley returned to his own estate in a rather
chastened mood. He had gone to visit Hugo's widow
prepared to dislike the woman excessively. Particularly since local gossip, as reported by his house-
keeper Mrs. Rumstead, pronounced her a cold, aloof
woman. But having met her, Pensley could not help
wondering how much of the problem was merely her
grief over the loss of both her parents as well as her
husband. For there was no doubt that something had
caused Mrs. Lawford to withdraw from the world.
That was a feeling Pensley knew only too well.

As he thought about it, his lordship realized there
was a quiet reserve about the lady he could not help
but like, and he reminded himself that Hugo had
never been a fool. Still, Richard found himself wondering how much of a hand this Mrs. Lawford had
had in the writing of Hugo's will, for there was no
doubt that it was most irregular for every bit of his
unentailed estate to go to this woman. Some, at least,
ought to have gone to his nephew for the upkeep of
those estates. Particularly as Hugo had told Pensley
he intended doing so when last they spoke, shortly
before both went on their respective journeys. It was
all so irregular.

Nevertheless, the matter could not have been said

to stand at the head of the list of Pensley's priorities. He had been gone close upon two years, and his estate showed the neglect. The bailiff he had left in charge was a good man but lacking in imagination as well as burdened with a reluctance to spend his master's money even when it was necessary. More than one of Pensley's tenants stood in need of a new roof, and several fences were in a shocking state of disrepair. As he rode, Pensley found himself wishing his wife, Sarah, were still alive. She was the one who had visited the tenants and always known how to put her finger on what was most needed. Even after four years he missed her very much.

Perhaps that was why he greeted Mrs. Arabella Fletcher with such a degree of warmth when he found her waiting for him in the drawing room. It was a very English room, quite as different from Hugo's drawing room as Arabella was different from Mrs. Lawford. She had been his wife's best friend and in the years since Sarah's death his friend as well. She had, in fact, been the first person to call upon Lord Pensley and his son upon their return from America. "Arabella! How do you do?" he asked, taking her hands briefly.

Another widow might have smiled wanly, but that was not for Mrs. Fletcher. "Well enough," she said briskly. "The last of the questions concerning my late husband's estate are finally settled."

"It has taken a long time," Pensley said with a frown.

Arabella nodded, a gesture that suited her. With a graceful wave of her hand she indicated the sofa and said, "Shall we sit? I confess this business has left me somewhat fatigued."

"Of course," he agreed quickly.

"Fletcher's family never liked me," Arabella went on matter-of-factly. "You know that as well as anyone. For years they blamed me that we had no children. And then, when Peter was finally born, just after Fletcher's death, they said he was not . . . not my husband's son. But he was. Fletcher never doubted it! But they used it as a pretext to challenge the will and Peter's inheritance."

"And?" Pensley prompted. "What finally decided the matter?"

At this point Arabella began to cry. "Philip Fletcher was such a *good* man," she said, forcing herself to speak in spite of the lump in her throat. "He knew the horrid things his family was saying, and it appears he knew, as well, how ill he was, though the rest of us had no notion. He wrote a letter, found just last week in the care of his solicitor and misplaced until now. In that letter Fletcher . . . Fletcher stated that the child I carried, three years ago, was his. That there was to be no doubt, legal or otherwise, as to the right of the child to bear his name and inherit that portion of the estate named in his will to go to his offspring."

There seemed nothing to say, and so Pensley waited as Arabella tried to compose herself.

"Silly of me, I know," she said at last, "but I cannot help being grateful to Fletcher. Not simply for assuring Peter's position, but for putting paid, once and for all, to their certainty, his family's, that Fletcher never loved me. But he did."

Pensley nodded, then said, "I am surprised, you know, that such a letter was needed. Surely anyone looking at the boy must see the resemblance to Philip. They both had the Fletcher nose and dark-brown eyes as well as curly dark hair. That could not have come from your side for you are all of you fair with gray eyes."

"Thank you," Arabella said warmly, "you are such a good friend to me. And what you say is true. I can only guess that Fletcher's family, having taken me in the greatest dislike, were not about to look at my son fairly. At any rate, it is all over now and I simply wanted to share my good news with you."

"How does Peter take this turn of events?" Pensley asked. "Is he here with you?"

Arabella contrived to laugh and shake her head at the same time. "No, he is at home in the care of his nanny. It is far too cold a day to drag him about. And in any event, at this age I am afraid he is not truly civilized enough to go visiting."

"I should not have minded," Pensley told her.

"I know you would not have; nevertheless, I thought it best to leave Peter home," Arabella told him. "As for how Peter is taking the news, well, what can a two-year-old understand of such matters? All he really understands is that Mommy isn't sad anymore. And Freddie? Is he content to be back in England again?"

Pensley smiled ruefully. "Oh, he is quite at home already. As if we had never left, in fact. This very day he called upon my neighbor, Hugo's widow, and managed to invite himself in for tea."

"Oh, dear," Arabella said. "Was Mrs. Lawford very angry?"

Pensley considered the matter. "I don't think she was angry at all," he answered finally. "That is what she said, and oddly enough I believe her."

"Probably hoping that if she ingratiates herself with the boy she might gain a foothold into your household and hence into your social circle," Arabella said with a distinct sniff. "That is, of course, unless she has already set her cap for you."

With a shake of his head Pensley said, "I think not. But in any event, it doesn't matter. I am merely grateful that Freddie has found someone to be kind to him and listen to his stories and answer all his questions. Particularly about India."

Arabella Fletcher was sufficiently wise to say nothing further. Instead, she turned the talk to other matters while she allowed Pensley to ring for refreshments.

Sometime later, when Mrs. Fletcher had left, Richard Pensley went looking for his son and found him, improbably, deeply engrossed in his studies with his tutor. For a moment Pensley watched the affecting tableau and then said abruptly, "Freddie, I wish to speak with you."

"Yes, Father," the boy replied, meeting Pensley's eyes with cheerful nonchalance.

Mr. Fargraves, the tutor, hastily rose. "Oh, my, yes, indeed. Of course, Master Alfred, we must take a break from our studies if your father wishes to speak with you. Shall I leave, sir?"

Pensley nodded. "Thank you, Fargraves. Perhaps you would care to take a short walk? For half an hour or so, if that is not too disruptive of your work? I confess myself somewhat surprised but undoubtedly pleased to see Freddie applying himself so well to his studies."

Mr. Fargraves smiled warmly. "Indeed he has been! I, too, am pleased, very pleased. Mind you, now, he shall never be a scholar, but I do not despair that we may yet make of him quite a creditably educated young gentleman. Ready for the finest schools in England, if you should so choose."

Pensley nodded, wisely ignoring his offspring's muttered, "I hope you don't!"

Instead, Lord Pensley said, "Excellent. Well, some outside air will do you good for a change from this stuffy classroom. I sometimes think we work you too hard, Fargraves."

The tutor permitted himself a brief laugh before he withdrew. Pensley decided to wait until the fellow had gone down the stairs before he spoke, and in the end it was Freddie who broke the silence. A trifle defiantly he said, "I didn't want to see her."

Startled, Pensley said, "Mrs. Lawford?"

"No, Mrs. Fletcher," Freddie retorted. Then, somewhat bewildered he said, "How did you know I'd seen Drusilla?"

"Because I called upon her myself," his father replied. "She told me about your visit. And you are to call her Mrs. Lawford," he added automatically.

"She didn't mind, did she?" Freddie asked anxiously. "She said she didn't, and I liked being there! Please say I may go again."

For a moment Pensley hesitated. "Mrs. Lawford is in mourning," he said, "and I shouldn't want to find you had been going over there to badger her for stories about India."

Hotly Freddie said, "I don't badger her, and I won't! She didn't mind me asking her about India. She said so! She's a right'un, not like . . . not like . . ."

Too late Freddie saw where his tongue was leading him. As did his father, who said, "Yes? Like who, Freddie? Like Mrs. Fletcher, whom you didn't wish to see?"

Scuffing the toe of his shoe, Freddie nodded. "It ain't that I don't like her," he said. "It's more that she don't like me. Forever saying I haven't any manners and such."

"Which is true," his father pointed out.

"Yes, but so what?" Freddie demanded hotly. "I don't see why I have to know how to primp and prance and do the pretty. It's all stupid anyway, isn't it? I've plenty of time before I shall have to do all that to ladies, haven't I? Besides, she just don't like me. It wouldn't matter if my manners were perfect, she still wouldn't like me."

"Alfred—" his father began warningly.

"It's true!" Freddie countered hotly. "I've heard her tell Mr. Fargraves she hasn't any use for children. None at all, she said."

"Mr. Fargraves?" Pensley asked, startled. "When would she have spoken to him?"

"He's a cousin of hers," Freddie replied impatiently. "She's the one who recommended him to be my tutor, remember?"

"Yes, of course," Pensley said with relief. "I had forgotten." Then, more sternly he added, "You ought not, however, to have been listening. Whatever you overheard, that does not excuse rudeness on your part."

"He tells her everything about you," Freddie persisted. "That's why she can always guess your plans."

"That will be quite enough," Lord Pensley said sternly. "We were speaking of rudeness."

"I won't be rude to her if she ain't rude to me," Freddie retorted.

Understanding very well the look of stubbornness on his son's face, Lord Pensley forbore to press the matter further. "Very well. I think it time now that you returned to your schoolwork and I to some business matters. How are your studies progressing?"

Happy to leave the subject and grateful that his father seemed to have forgotten about Mrs. Lawford, Freddie was eager to talk about something else. Anything else. Lord Pensley, for his part, listened with a keen ear as Freddie vented his frustration at some of the subjects Mr. Fargrave considered essential to a young gentleman's education. He did not, however, agree to change that course of study and with some relief relinquished his son back into the tutor's capable hands. Mr. Fargraves, in turn, looked much refreshed by his walk.

Pensley then went to the library and the papers that waited there for him. Including certain documents that required his signature concerning Mrs. Lawford's inheritance. He also made a mental note to be careful of what was spoken in front of Mr. Fargraves.

4

About a week later Alfred Pensley was ushered into the morning room, where Drusilla Lawford sat writing a letter. Putting aside the delicately japanned desk, Mrs. Lawford held out a welcoming hand and said, "Hello, Freddie! How are you today? Escaped from your tutor, I see."

Freddie flushed. "Yes, but I did learn that passage in Latin first. Even Mr. Fargraves said I deserved the rest of the day off for that!"

Drusilla smiled approvingly. She was afraid that Lord Pensley did not altogether like Freddie's visits to her house, even though he allowed them, and she had contrived to make it clear to Freddie that he was not to neglect his studies in order to visit her. She stopped short, however, of asking if Lord Pensley had forbidden Freddie's visits. Reprehensible of her, no doubt, but if her fears had been confirmed, she would have felt obliged to tell Freddie he must obey his father and Drusilla found she did not want to do that.

Drusilla did not know that she had mistaken Lord Pensley. She only knew that she liked the boy and that Hugo had liked him as well. It also touched her that Freddie was so very keen on India. Recollecting her own two brothers, she wanted to give Freddie as clear a picture of India as possible so that if, in the end, he did go there, he would at least know what it was he was facing.

With a smile Drusilla said approvingly, "Excellent! However useless Latin may appear to you now, you will be grateful for it later. That is splendid news. Now I have some news for you. I am going to London, later this week, perhaps. Hugo's sister-in-law has asked me to come and visit her, and I think I shall."

"Don't want you to go," Freddie said resolutely. "Want you to stay and marry m'father."

Somewhat taken aback, Drusilla laughed. "My dear Freddie, however long I might stay here, I doubt very much your father and I would marry."

"Why not?" Freddie persisted.

With a sinking heart Drusilla realized that it had not been a kindness, after all, to let the boy come and weave his fantasies about her. Gently she said, with an air of finality, "Because your father and I would never suit. Never."

Whether it was true or not, Drusilla would not allow herself to wonder, for the most important thing was to stop Freddie from imagining something that would hurt very much if it never happened. As for her own dreams about Lord Pensley, well, that was all they were. He had not come to call since that first visit, sending round the few papers that needed her attention. No doubt he had concluded that, though she was not a predatory harpy, she was a dull and quiet widow who held not the least interest for such a fashionable memeber of the *ton*.

Freddie could find nothing to say and Drusilla was grateful when she heard Witton's footsteps approaching the morning room. Opening the door, he announced, "Mrs. Arabella Fletcher."

Drusilla moved forward to greet her guest with a smile. "How nice of you to call, Mrs. Fletcher," she said.

In a soft voice Arabella replied, "I thought I ought to come and call upon you, Mrs. Lawford. We are, after all, both of us widows, and can therefore understand each other's distress so well."

"You are very kind," Drusilla said with some surprise. "Please come in and meet another neighbor who comes to visit me. Freddie, make your bow to Mrs. Fletcher. Surely you are acquainted?"

Young Pensley made a curt bow to Arabella, then said a trifle breathlessly, "I must be going, Mrs. Lawford. My studies, you know."

Drusilla agreed while Arabella said nothing. When he was gone, however, Mrs. Fletcher observed, "The child is in strong need of a mother to take him in hand. His lack of manners is quite shocking."

Mrs. Lawford said nothing, determined not to cross swords with the first real visitor she had had in some time. "Won't you be seated?" she said. "Shall I ring for tea?"

"Thank you, I should like that," Arabella replied as she took a seat beside her hostess on the couch. "I had meant to call upon you before, but the roads are so impossible these winter months."

Drusilla did not trouble to remind her that she had been in residence through the summer as well. Instead she said, "I am delighted to have you. It has, I confess, been a trifle lonely here. My brothers and their wives are still in India, the rest of my family scattered about England, and I have not yet met Hugo's."

Mrs. Fletcher nodded with a satisfied air. "And we

have not been precisely welcoming hereabouts, have we?" She did not wait for a reply but went on, "You must know it was never expected that Hugo would marry. That has been one count against you. The other is that you are new. Even now, after almost ten years I am considered scarcely more than an upstart. That is why I came to call."

She paused as a maid entered the room with the tea tray and waited until the girl was gone and Drusilla had poured out a cup before she went on. "We ought to be allies, I thought. We are much alike, after all. Both widows. Both without close family. Both rather alone here. I don't suppose you have a child?"

Drusilla shook her head. "No. Hugo and I were married but a short time, you know, before he died."

"How dreadful for you," Arabella said sympathetically. "I only asked because I have a child, Peter, who is not yet three. If you also had a child, that might have been one more bond between us. Well, never mind, we shall become fast friends without that. Tell me, does Lord Pensley's son come here often?"

Drusilla hesitated, not wishing to cause trouble for Freddie, and yet she had not been brought up to lie. In the end she evaded the question. "He is a good boy, and for Hugo's sake I cannot bear to turn him away," Drusilla said gently. "Indeed, for his own sake. Freddie has, I fear, an exaggerated notion of what it means to be in India, and I should like him to begin to understand that it is not the endless wonderful adventure he appears to believe it would be."

"I see," Arabella replied thoughtfully. "And is it Lord Pensley who brings him?"

Drusilla laughed. "No, he comes on his own. If Lord Pensley were to call upon me so often, I fear I should die of the shock!"

"Why?" Arabella asked quickly.

"Because I fear he does not entirely approve of me," Drusilla answered frankly. "He thinks Hugo never meant to wed and therefore ought not to have."

"Tell me, what do you think of Lord Pensley?" Arabella asked carefully. Drusilla hesitated, and Arabella added coaxingly, "Come, tell me, Mrs. Lawford. I give you my word I shan't pass on what you say."

Coming to a decision, Drusilla set down her teacup and said, "Very well. I find him a man too much accustomed to having his own way about things. Very quick to judge, though willing, perhaps, to give way should he discover himself to be mistaken. The rub is that I should think one would find it very difficult to persuade him he was wrong!"

All of which, Drusilla thought grimly, was true. But the words told what she thought of Lord Pensley, not what she felt. That was quite a different matter. Nor did she say that she thought his lordship would be the kind of man one could speak to about many things. Instinct warned her this visitor did not wish to hear Lord Pensley praised. Not by her.

"Do you find him handsome?" Arabella persisted.

This time Drusilla did not hesitate. "He would be if he could ever be brought to smile," she said. "Instead, one has the feeling he almost never does. That because of either an elevated sense of his own importance or bitterness at the world, he never feels the need to put himself out for anyone."

"In short, you dislike him?" Arabella asked eagerly.

Drusilla met her guest's eyes squarely. "In short, I am no danger to you," she said bluntly, feeling the by-now-familiar ache inside. "That is why I have answered your questions about Lord Pensley, however impertinent I may have found them. Because I thought perhaps that was why you had come to call upon me today: to assure yourself you need not fear me as a rival."

For a moment matters hung in the balance, then Arabella smiled a wintry smile. "That is frank enough, at all events. Very well, since we have taken the gloves off, let me admit that that was indeed my reason for calling today."

"And?" Drusilla asked. "What is your conclu-usion?"

This time Arabella smiled a more genuine smile as her eyes raked over her hostess from head to toe. "My conclusion is that while we will never be rivals, we may become friends. I am relieved to hear your opinion of Lord Pensley, although naturally I cannot entirely enter into it. But even had you professed a *tendre* for the poor fellow, I should have been reassured. Someone told me you were pretty. And so I suppose you are, in a rather unremarkable way. But scarcely a threat to me. Lord Pensley's tastes run to more fashionable ladies and more classic features."

"Such as yours?" Drusilla hazarded.

Arabella inclined her head. "Such as mine," she agreed. "You should have seen Lord Pensley's first wife. We might have been sisters, she and I. No, I have nothing to fear here."

"How delightful to know that," Drusilla replied
ironically.

Arabella laughed. "That, my dear, is precisely why
I think we shall be friends," she said. "You are the
first woman to take up residence hereabouts with
whom I feel I may speak frankly. You will not betray
me, nor I you, and we may say precisely what we
think. You've no notion how tedious it is to spend all
one's time with worthy, eminently worthy, ladies
who seem never to have laughed in their lives. And
who think one is beyond the pale if one does. What a
pity you will not be in London for the Season. But
then, perhaps that sort of thing does not interest you
very much? I shall be leaving in a week or two for
London, but I promise we shall renew our acquaintance as soon as I return. We shall be friends!"

Through all of this Drusilla held her counsel.
Another woman might have been so offended that
she would have said so. Drusilla did not. Perhaps it
was instinct that told her silence was the safest
route. So Drusilla smiled briefly, but she held back
the information that she, too, would be going to
London for the Season.

Arabella Fletcher left a short time later in excellent spirits, and Drusilla saw her to her carriage.
As it drove out of sight, Drusilla slowly reclimbed
the steps, her cloak pulled tightly closed around her,
a wry smile upon her lips. Once back inside the
house, she handed the cloak to a footman and went to
the library. There she took a deep breath and rang
for Witton and his wife. It was time to put his lordship out of her mind; madness to dwell upon
someone she had spoken with no more than once.
Much to her relief, Witton and his wife did not
dawdle.

"Yes, Madam?" he asked with a bow as his wife curtsied beside him.

Drusilla clasped her hands on the desk in front of her. "I feel a trifle foolish about this," she confessed briskly, "for I know you had charge of the house while Mr. Lawford was in India, but there are a number of instructions I should like to give for while I am in London."

Witton coughed discreetly. "As to that, madam, may I assure you we shall welcome them. Mr. Lawford was a most excellent gentleman but lacked, shall we say, the knowledge of a lady of the manor as to what needs seeing to when the master or mistress is away."

Drusilla smiled warmly. "Precisely. Now here is what I should like done. . . ."

Half an hour later, Drusilla mounted the stairs to the second floor, feeling herself to be in excellent spirits. If matters went just as smoothly with the packing, there could be nothing more to wish for except a lack of snow on the journey itself. For in spite of her initial misgivings at going to London and accepting the hospitality of Hugo's sister-in-law, Drusilla felt a rising excitement. She had never more than passed through London, never had a Season, and somehow felt almost as giddy as a schoolgirl at the notion. Though she would of course limit her social activities. The year of mourning might have ended, but Drusilla could not yet feel it was proper to enter into a full round of festivities.

Upon leaving the Lawford house Arabella Fletcher drove straight round to see Lord Pensley. It was, she had decided, her duty to tell Richard just how much time his son was spending at Mrs. Lawford's home.

Not that she bore Drusilla any malice in the matter;
in fact, Arabella genuinely thought she would be
grateful not to have the child hanging about all the
time.

In excellent spirits she mounted the steps and
greeted the footman, who knew her well, with a
request to see Lord Pensley. He was in the library
and Arabella followed the footman, assuring the
fellow she did not mind a bit being received there. At
the sight of her Pensley set down his pen and said
with a smile, "Arabella! How delightful to see you."

She moved forward to meet him halfway. "I can
only stay a moment, Richard, and only because I saw
something today I thought I ought to tell you about."

Quickly Pensley searched her face for signs of
distress but found none. He would have said, in fact,
that she seemed very happy. "What is it?" he asked.

"I called upon Mrs. Lawford today," Arabella said.

Now, why in God's name, Pensley demanded
silently of himself, should that woman's name cause
him to start so? Why should an image of her face,
lined with care, rise so clearly before him? She was
his responsibility, nothing more, so why did she
haunt his dreams?

"Well?" Pensley prompted, a trifle impatiently,
when Arabella hesitated. "Did you dislike her?"

Mrs. Fletcher shook her head decisively. "No,
quite the contrary. I think she is something of an
original and far more likely to be amusing than some
milk-and-water chit, even if she is rather provincial.
No, I wished to speak to you about Alfred. He was
visiting Mrs. Lawford, and from something she said I
gather he goes there frequently. I simply wished to
be sure you were aware of the situation. She did not
precisely say so, but I thought she had perhaps be-

gun to grow tired of Alfred's constant visits. It cannot be fair to Mrs. Lawford to have him hanging about all the time."

"Good God, no. I should think she would have enough to distress her without that. And she is far too kind to send him away if he does prove a nuisance," Pensley agreed readily. He paused and added, "I think it is as well I had planned to leave for London soon. Perhaps I shall take Freddie and Fargraves with me. There is no reason he cannot study there as easily as here, and Fargraves can show him about the city. I think he might enjoy that."

"An excellent notion," Arabella said approvingly. "Well, I shall go now. I had not meant to stop at all except that I thought I should drop a hint in your ear of Alfred's activities. Particularly as I did not think Mrs. Lawford would be resolute enough to do so."

"That was kind of you," Pensley told her warmly. Then, taking her hand, he asked, "When do you leave for London?"

"Within the week," Arabella said with great satisfaction. "Now that the matter of Peter's legitimacy is established, I've no need to count farthings. The trustees have been generous while the issue was in doubt, but that is not the same as holding the purse strings oneself, after all!" She paused, then colored becomingly as she asked, "When do you leave for London?"

"Within the week," Pensley echoed her.

5

Drusilla's first sight of London made her shudder, but that was not entirely the fault of the city. Two days on the road had shortened her temper considerably in spite of the comfort of Hugo's well-sprung carriage. Contrary to her hopes, there had been snow to make the roads treacherous, and the inns she had stayed at overnight had been over-crowded because of the poor weather and her sheets had been damp. Now dark clouds loomed over the city of London and promised more snow.

It was not, Drusilla reflected to herself, that she was unaccustomed to noise and dirt and crowding. No one who had lived in India could be. Nevertheless she could not deny that her first sight of London was a disappointing one. As though the city had dressed in its oldest clothes rather than a gay ball gown to meet her. And what else did you expect? she demanded of herself. Who are you that London should cater to your wishes?

Perhaps it was the contrast that made the Lawford townhouse appear so welcoming. From the moment Drusilla stepped across the threshold, warmth and acceptance seemed to envelop her. The footman who took her fur-trimmed winter pelisse of favorite blue and her fur muff had smiled as he led her to the drawing room, where Mrs. Lawford had instantly risen to her feet to take Drusilla's hands in her own. It was an elegant room furnished with gilded tables and fashionable if not entirely comfortable chairs and sofas. Mrs. Lawford herself was young. Not more than five-and-forty and fashionably gowned in a robe of purple crepe that did nothing to diminish her attractiveness while it still conveyed that she was in half-mourning. A neat widow's cap of lace sat on her dark curls and a slim figure of moderate height completed the impression of elegance.

"How do you do, Drusilla?" Mrs. Lawford asked, still holding her hands. "Come in and sit by the fire beside me, my dear, and please call me Elizabeth. I am persuaded you must welcome a good blaze after your journey. How were the roads?"

"Tolerable," Drusilla said, doing as she was bid. "I might wish they had not been so icy, however."

"It is a wonder you did not overturn in the snow," Elizabeth said with a shudder. "A horrible time of year to travel, but fortunately you are safely here and I cannot tell you how much I welcome your company."

"You are very kind," Drusilla said, coloring. "I know Hugo's marriage must have seemed odd to you, and I should not have blamed you had you wished not to acknowledge me at all."

"Well, that is plain speaking," her hostess observed. "But I should not be so frank with other people, my dear, they might not understand. Or they might choose to use it against you. But as for not acknowledging you—why, there could be no question of that! Hugo was my brother-in-law and a more levelheaded fellow I cannot imagine. Whatever his reasons for marrying you, they must have been excellent. No, I am merely grateful that he gave me a sister-in-law at last! I am sure we shall deal famously together. And now you must have some tea. I am persuaded nothing could be more desirable to you right now."

Drusilla laughed. "You are quite correct, of course. I have been wishing for some these past thirty miles. Indeed, for these past two days. Somehow tea at an inn is never quite the same as in a home."

"How very true," Elizabeth agreed. She paused as the maid entered and she gave the necessary orders, then turned once more to her guest. "I fear I must apologize for my son, Julian. He ought to have been here to greet you, and he is not. You know how young men are, forever at their own amusements!"

Drusilla hesitated, then plunged in boldly. "It is not, perhaps, that he blames me for inheriting what he must himself have expected?" As her hostess stared, Drusilla blundered on, "I should not blame him if he did, I should just like to know."

"Well there you are out," Elizabeth Lawford said briskly "My son is not precisely a pauper, for he did inherit the entire entailed estates. And our family was scarcely impoverished before that. No, Julian bears you no ill will for his uncle's wishes. As he has so often said to me, Hugo had a perfect right to leave his money, wherever he chose. No, you will find Julian quite as eager to welcome you to the family as I am myself."

Drusilla smiled. "How fortunate I am to have such a generous new family. But then Hugo was so kind I should have had difficulty imagining it otherwise."

"On the contrary," Elizabeth contradicted her firmly, "I should say that we were the fortunate ones!"

The maid entered with the tea, and Mrs. Lawford busied herself with pouring out and handing her young guest a plate of cakes and cookies. "You must recoup your strength," Elizabeth told her guest playfully, "if you expect to keep up with the round of balls and routs and breakfasts and such that we attend here in London."

"Oh, but . . ." Drusilla broke off in confusion.

"What is it, my dear?" Elizabeth asked kindly.

"Well, I had not expected . . . I did not come prepared. . . ." Once more Drusilla stumbled over her words.

"You did not expect to lead such a gay life here?" Elizabeth suggested with some surprise. "But why ever not? Surely you must know the Season has just begun and we do move in the best circles."

"I-I know," Drusilla conceded. "It is just that . . . that it has been only a little more than a year since Hugo died. I had not thought it would be entirely proper to-to—"

"To become a social butterfly?" Elizabeth hazarded. "Nonsense!" she said, putting her teacup down with a thump. "Your feelings do you credit, of course, but Hugo would never have wanted you to stay at home and mope like this. He would have said you should go about and enjoy yourself, and to the devil with what anyone may think!"

Elizabeth did such a clever imitation of her brother-in-law's voice that Drusilla could not help but laugh. "You are right," she conceded. "That is just what Hugo would have said."

"Good. Then we will have no more of this nonsense about mourning," Elizabeth said firmly.

"Yes, but I still haven't the proper clothes," Drusilla objected. "However much I might want to accompany you to balls and such, I simply can't."

"Not yet," Elizabeth conceded, "but very soon. We will visit Mademoiselle Suzette tomorrow and she will produce a complete wardrobe more quickly than you might think. Then, my dear, I shall introduce you to everyone, and everyone will be charmed just as I am."

Drusilla was wondering how to respond to this kind speech when the doors to the drawing room opened and a young man strolled into the room. He could not have been, Drusilla supposed, more than five-and-twenty but he moved with a careless self-assurance one might have expected in an older man. From the tip of his polished boots to the fitted pantaloons to elegant coat and intricately tied neckcloth, everything bespoke the gentleman of leisure. His features were regular and made more pleasing by the smile that came so easily to his face and the cap of dark curls that shaped his head so handsomely. Even had his fond mother not cried out, "Julian!" Drusilla would have had no difficulty placing the family resemblance.

"Mama," the fellow said, coming forward to greet his mother with a swift embrace, "will you introduce me to your guest?"

"Fie upon you," Elizabeth said with a smile, "how can you not realize that this is your Uncle Hugo's wife, Drusilla?"

Astonished, Julian Lawford bowed and took his new aunt's hand. Without relinquishing it, he said playfully, "You must forgive me, ma'am, but it never crossed my mind that you might be Hugo's widow."

"Why not?" Drusilla asked, her curiosity aroused.

"Because," Julian said with unabashed gallantry, "you are far too pretty. And far too young to have been Hugo's wife. Oh, no, please don't misunderstand, I don't fault you. Quite the contrary. I think Hugo was a lucky fellow, indeed! I only wish I had known he had such a pretty wife, for I should certainly not have left it until now to make your acquaintance."

Drusilla felt herself color under this kind attention and she opened her mouth to halt the flow of pretty compliments. Elizabeth was before her, however, and said, "Hush, Julian! Drusilla will think you deal only in Spanish coin if you do not stop."

"Spanish coin?" Julian retorted indignantly. "Nothing of the sort! But I fear my mother may be right that I am distressing you, so I shall say no more, Mrs. Lawford." He paused, then laughed ruefully. "Or should I call you Aunt Drusilla? Yes, I think I shall do that. Unless you object, of course. It is so delightfully absurd, you see."

Drusilla looked at Elizabeth helplessly. Her hostess laughed also and said after a moment, "Julian is right, it is absurd. But what is he to call you if not Aunt Drusilla? *Shall* you mind?"

Drusilla shook her head decisively. "No, for I, too, find it amusing."

"Good," Elizabeth said approvingly. Then, turning to her son, she said sternly, "I shall expect you to accompany us about, Julian, and escort your aunt to the theater and such. No doubt you will find it all a dead bore, but Drusilla has spent such a long time in India that she shall need some time to find her feet here among the *ton*. And I shall depend upon you,

Julian, to help me keep the gazetted fortune-hunters
away from her. She has not the experience, isolated
as she must have been in India, of being surrounded
by admirers as I have no doubt she will be in
London." Abruptly Elizabeth turned to her guest and
said, "I hope you do not mind plain speaking, my
dear, but I thought it best to enlist Julian's aid at
once. Then he cannot cry off and it is always so much
more comfortable to have a gentleman to squire one
about that I could not resist dragooning him for the
purpose."

It occurred to Drusilla that her hostess had a very
odd notion of life in India. Frankly she doubted that
London would provide her with more suitors than
had an isolated military camp in India that never had
enough young ladies to occupy the attention of all
the young men. It was not in her to boast, however,
about such things, so she merely smiled and said to
her nephew, "I should be grateful, indeed, for your
kindness."

"Good," Julian echoed his mother. "When do we
begin? Tonight?"

With a wry expression Elizabeth said, "Unless I am
much mistaken, Drusilla would far prefer a warm
bed tonight than a drafty theater, for I collect that is
where you planned to take her. Time enough for
going about in a few days."

"As you wish"—Julian shrugged—"and frankly
just as well. I would have done it, had you asked, but
that would have meant crying off from playing cards
tonight, which is what I should much rather do. Not
that you are not charming, Aunt Drusilla, it is simply
that I owe Tom Ravenscraft the chance to beat me."

"Do you think he shall?" Elizabeth asked doubtfully.

Julian smiled. "No, but he wouldn't thank me for denying him the chance to try. Ah, well, such is life. I must be off now, to change into evening clothes. I expect we'll look in at White's later on. Welcome to London, Aunt Drusilla."

The two women watched him leave and then Elizabeth turned to her guest and said, "He is a delightful boy, but a sad rapscallion, I fear."

"Nonsense," Drusilla replied stoutly, "I should say he merely has the high spirits a young gentleman his age ought to have."

"Well, I think so," Elizabeth confided, "but it would never do for me to admit it to the boy. He would never give me a moment's peace if I did!"

Drusilla laughed and the talk turned to the pleasant topic of fashions and fabrics and pattern books, and she began to feel more at peace than she had for some time.

6

On the evening of the Earl of Ormsby's party, Drusilla found herself stricken with an unaccustomed trepidation. Particularly when she regarded herself in the mirror. Never had she owned a gown as fashionable as the one designed by Mademoiselle Suzette, and the knowledge that a good many more hung in her closet did nothing to quiet her fears. Nor did it help that even Elizabeth had expressed concern when Mademoiselle Suzette first proposed its design. "Shan't they think Drusilla sadly encroaching to puff herself off in such a way?" she had hesitantly asked.

Mademoiselle Suzette had drawn herself up to her full height and replied, "Me, I do not choose to make the widow dowdy. If that is what you wish, go to somewhere else."

"Nothing of the sort," Mrs. Lawford had said hastily. "It is just that there will be talk of Drusilla's marriage, and one would not wish to encourage that."

"Talk? Pah!" Mademoiselle Suzette shook her head. "No, you wish everyone to say, hah! Monsieur Hugo had much sense marrying madame."

In the end Elizabeth and Drusilla had been persuaded and Mademoiselle Suzette had been given free rein to indulge her creative genius. The result was a confection of wine-colored silk and lace that contrived to convey the notion Drusilla was a widow, but a very dashing one. Pale gloves and slippers of the same color completed the toilette while diamonds circled Drusilla's neck and dropped from her ears. Her hair was swept up and back and threaded with ribbons of wine and silver lace.

Drusilla turned to her maid. "Will it do, Annie?" she asked.

Annie smiled sourly. "Aye, it will do. You'll be the smartest lady there, ma'am. And a good thing, too. I'm not one to be thinking you should hide yourself in shabby colors, pretending to be an antidote, offensive to no one. If that was what you wanted, ma'am, you would have done better to stay at Mr. Lawford's country house." She paused and added, apparently irrelevantly, "I make no doubt his lordship would like it."

Coloring, Drusilla spoke sharply, "That will be enough, Annie. I must go and show Mrs. Lawford."

Annie dropped a demure curtsy, but neither woman was deceived and Drusilla hastily left the room. Elizabeth and Julian were already downstairs waiting. "My dear aunt, you look *ravissante*," he said gallantly.

"So she does," Elizabeth agreed, resplendent herself in a gown of silver crepe, "even if it is not entirely proper of you to say so, Julian. Come, let us go in to dinner. I wish to arrive late but not so late we will be lost in the crush."

Both mother and son kept up such a steady stream of nonsense that Drusilla had no time to give in to a fit of nerves, even had she wanted to. Nor could she help being touched when, as they were about to leave, Julian presented her with an elegant ivory fan to carry. "Merely a bit of trumpery, Aunt Drusilla," he said carelessly when she tried to thank him, "but I thought you might like it."

Then there was no time to talk as the footman was holding out their cloaks and the coachman opening the door to the carriage. En route Elizabeth told her about the more important members of the *ton* Drusilla was likely to meet, and suddenly, or so it seemed, they had arrived. Or, at any rate, they reached the line of carriages waiting to leave off the guests to the party.

Once inside, there was something of a wait again before the three were presented to their host and hostess, but Julian beguiled the time by pointing out to Drusilla all the people his mother had been telling her about. And Elizabeth was all agog at the number of flowers that had been ordered to adorn the tables and alcoves and stairs and corners of the rooms. Drusilla was far more impressed by the paintings that seemed to literally cover all the walls of the house. Finally, however, they reached the top of the staircase. "Countess, may I present Mrs. Lawford? My brother-in-law's widow. And my son, Julian, of course."

The Countess of Ormsby inclined her head graciously and replied, "You have but recently returned from India, is that correct, Mrs. Lawford?"

"I returned a year ago, your grace, shortly after my husband's death," Drusilla said as she met her hostess's eyes.

"And do you enjoy being back in England?" the countess asked.

"Very much so," Drusilla replied with a smile,

"particularly as Hugo's sister and nephew have been so kind to me."

The countess nodded and then turned to the next arrivals, leaving the Lawfords free to proceed into one of the rooms behind her. As they did so, Julian could not resist pressing Drusilla's hand and whispering, "Well done, Auntie!"

"Indeed, my dear," Elizabeth seconded, "Hugo would have been proud of you. Very proud, indeed." Then briskly she said, "I shall leave you now. Cards are my passion and I've no doubt I shall find my bosom bows already at their tables. Enjoy yourselves, my dears."

She headed off in the direction of a small bookroom and Drusilla turned instinctively to Julian. He smiled and said, "I shan't desert you. Not unless you tell me to, but even then I should prefer to introduce you about."

"Thank you, I should like that," she answered with a sigh of relief.

With no trouble Julian seemed to find the room where all the young bloods of the *ton* had gathered, and Drusilla soon found herself surrounded by a crowd of admirers. Sir Peter Dunsworth, Lord Weatherby, Edmond Radbourne, Lord Farnham, Mr. Jason Thornley, Mr. Percy Braden, and half a dozen other kind gentlemen had all professed themselves eager to dance attendance upon her. It was a heady experience and it did not occur to her to wonder why he had introduced her to no ladies.

Somewhat to her surprise, for she had heard that the gentlemen of the *ton* were frippery fellows, Drusilla also found herself answering questions about India.

"The uprising in 1806 *was* our fault," she insisted. "None of our officers seemed to understand the importance to the sepoys of retaining their beards and headdress and caste marks."

"Doesn't do to coddle these fellows," someone countered. "Heathens, the lot of them. What we really need is to send out more missionaries. Civilize them, at the very least. Haven't I heard that they burn widows there?"

"Yes, they do sometimes burn widows," Drusilla agreed. Then, forcing herself to smile lightly, she added, "And I will concede that when my husband died I was very grateful not to be an Indian woman expected to immolate myself on his funeral pyre."

"There you are, then," her questioner said triumphantly. "Need to civilize them. Send more missionaries or something."

Drusilla shook her head. "That won't do the trick," she retorted. "Since the Charter of 1813 there have been missionaries in India. Indeed, my own father was a clergyman. But I cannot say that he was greeted with enthusiasm there. Oh, they liked him well enough as a man, but as a missionary. . . . Well, how would you feel if someone from Persia came and tried to convert you to belief in the Koran?"

"My dear Mrs. Lawford, that is scarcely the same thing," Sir Peter Dunsworth protested.

"Isn't it?" Drusilla asked. "Why not? I can assure you that to someone in India the distinction would be quite lost."

At that moment a voice cut in to say, "Mrs. Lawford, I felicitate you. I was not aware that you were in the habit of giving lectures in the midst of routs."

Drusilla looked up, startled to find Lord Pensley

staring at her. A large painting of a previous Earl of Ormsby hung behind his shoulder and the effect was almost overwhelming; she blinked. But Lord Pensley's unexpectedly gentle smile robbed the words of offense. Another voice, Mrs. Fletcher's, was not so kind. "What an utter bore!" she said, yawning politely.

A wave of vertigo seized Drusilla and she found herself answering almost at random. "Good evening, Lord Pensley. Mrs. Fletcher. How delightful to see you again. You are quite right, however. This is far too weighty a topic for a party." Realizing how absurd she sounded, Drusilla paused, took a deep breath, and went on more sedately, "Someone must tell me, instead, what I ought to see in London."

Lord Pensley raised an eyebrow in mock salute. Arabella merely raised in eyebrow. The one thought that sustained Drusilla was the knowledge that Mrs. Fletcher's silk gown was of a far drearier shade of wine than her own. As she fought a sense of helplessness, Julian Lawford move closer. "We are shocking fellows," he announced protectively. "Not one of us has thought to procure Mrs. Lawford a glass of champagne."

Instantly several of the gentlemen offered to do so, and Julian selected one at random to honor with the task. Drusilla met his eyes and hastily suppressed a giddy desire to laugh as he winked at her. "My gallant knight to the rescue?" she murmured.

He bowed. From the corner of her eyes Drusilla saw Lord Pensley and Arabella Fletcher move away, and she felt the tension ease from her shoulders. Why he should have produced such a sensation in her was madness to consider. But now that Lord

Pensley had withdrawn, Drusilla could again think and speak intelligently and the men around her vied to carry out her wishes.

"You must let me take you to see the Tower of London."

"No, Astley's Amphitheater and I shall take her!"

"Well, she must surely grant me the opportunity to take her for a drive in Hyde Park."

"I am determined I shall be the one to give her her first sight of the Serpentine!"

"And I shall take her 'round to Vauxhall Gardens."

And so it went. All very pleasant nonsense, Drusilla had to admit, and if her eyes strayed more than was wise to a certain pair of shoulders and watched who he spoke with, well, who was to know? She ought, she told herself sternly, to be grateful the fellow was ignoring her if he set her insides to churning so! But she was not. Indeed, she felt almost indecently pleased when at last he did come around again and dextrously separated her from her circle of admirers by claiming a need to talk business. This time there was no Mrs. Fletcher at his side.

"Business? At a party?" Farnham demanded incredulously.

"Unfair, patently unfair!" Dunsworth added with a smile.

Pensley merely shrugged. "The hazards, and benefits, of being named the trustee for an attractive widow such as Mrs. Lawford. Don't worry, I shall return her to all of you shortly and you may all continue to try to impress her with your grace and wisdom and town polish. Mrs. Lawford?"

With a laugh Drusilla took the proffered arm. When Lord Pensley had somehow found a corner, deserted save for the flowers and the hunting party depicted in the large painting above the sofa, she asked sensibly, "What was this estate business you needed to speak to me about? I cannot conceive of anything that could not have waited until morning." Abruptly she frowned. "Is it Witton? Or one of the other servants? Hurt or ill?"

Pensley placed a soothing hand over her tremulous ones. "No, Mrs. Lawford, nothing of the sort. I am sorry, I had not thought to alarm you this way."

"Then, what is the matter?" she demanded.

Pensley hesitated. How to explain an impulse he did not even understand? His upbringing stood him in good stead, however, and after a moment he was once more the polished gentleman.

"Will you be angry," he asked with a careless air, "if I confess that I haven't any business to discuss? That I merely wanted to be able to rescue you from that circle of fellows and sit with you myself?"

"Now you are roasting me," she told him with a frown.

"Not a bit of it," he replied with innocent eyes. "You looked a trifle fatigued and in need of respite."

"Such kindness!" She grinned. "You had best be careful, however, or all this unaccustomed attentiveness will no doubt go to my head and I shall become insufferable."

"Impossible," he retorted gallantly. Again the warmth crept into his voice then and chased away the mockery as he went on, "Why is it so difficult to believe my motives were of the kindest? I did think that you needed to be rescued, earlier, when you were talking about India."

"You were quite right," Drusilla conceded ruefully. "Unfortunately I seem unable to guard my tongue when the subject of India arises. As usual, I almost landed myself in the briars."

"What you said tonight sounded very sensible to me," Pensley observed coolly.

Drusilla laughed. "Sensible! You might as well call me a bluestocking and ruin me forever."

"At any rate, Hugo would have been proud of you," Pensley countered.

That silenced Drusilla. After a moment she said, "I should like to think so. Nor, I confess, do I really wish to stop trying to rid people of the nonsensical notions they have about India. But now I shall be uncivil and change the subject. How is Freddie?"

There was a rueful look about Pensley's eyes as he replied, "My son? Do you know, Mrs. Lawford, I begin to suspect that I find you in London simply because you know him to be here. Certainly that you prefer his company to mine."

"Not prefer it, precisely," Drusilla countered, "but he *is* a delightful boy."

For a moment there was no tension between them. Then Pensley said, "I had not known you were coming to London until I saw you here tonight. Where are you staying?"

"With Hugo's sister-in-law and nephew, Elizabeth and Julian Lawford," she replied eagerly. "You cannot imagine how kind they have been to me."

Richard was silent. After a moment he said lightly, once more the polite stranger, "I see. Well, I hope you enjoy your stay in London."

"I shall," Drusilla assured him. Then, with a frown, she asked "Have I offended you somehow?"

"Certainly not," he replied coolly. "It is no business of mine where you stay or what your plans have been. I am pleased to know you are content. And now I must relinquish you," he said as a number of Drusilla's suitors came straight toward them. He paused, then added, almost against his will, it seemed, "Should you ever need my help, Mrs. Lawford, in any way you know you may always call upon me for assistance."

Drusilla had no time to answer or even to wonder at the warmth with which his lordship spoke. Already a number of gentlemen had reached them.

"Fair is fair," Dunsworth said with mock sternness. "You have had your chat, Pensley, and now we are here to claim Mrs. Lawford's attention once more."

Richard rose, bowed, and with a lazy smile gracefully retired, leaving Drusilla to find herself once more engaged in heady bantering. That smile prompted more than one comment. "I vow," Farnham told her, "you have thawed Pensley. We are quite overcome with admiration."

All very delightful, she insisted again, this time aloud, as Julian handed her into the carriage so the three could return home sometime later.

"*Such* a success!" Elizabeth roasted her as the horses began to move.

Drusilla chuckled wryly. "And no doubt it would go straight to my head and make me completely insufferable were it not for the fact that one cannot help but be aware that the Season has scarcely begun and that most of the young girls to make their come-out this year have not yet arrived."

From a dark corner of the carriage Julian said, "I must disagree, Aunt Drusilla. Were this the height of the Season you must still have created a circle of admirers for yourself. For however you may view yourself, you are a wealthy young widow. And a beautiful one. Among the *ton*, where such things are a preoccupation, you could not help but be noticed. Did you see, by the by, Lord Pensley with Mrs. Fletcher? One hears an engagement is expected by the end of the Season."

Drusilla did not answer at once and Elizabeth asked her, "Is something wrong, my dear?"

"No, I am only a little tired," Drusilla replied as she leaned back against the squabs.

"And everything is still rather strange to you?" Elizabeth hazarded.

Drusilla smiled at her hostess warmly. "How well you understand," she said. "Yes, it is all strange to me. Even the part about being Hugo's widow. My marriage to your brother scarcely seems real sometimes."

"That is only to be expected," Elizabeth told her guest stoutly. "Had Hugo been able to give you a child before he died, things might have been different. But as it is, you had such a short time together. It is no wonder that you do not feel properly his wife and even less his widow."

"There was no child, I take it?" Julian asked, leaning forward.

Drusilla shook her head. "As your mother said, we were married such a short time."

To herself, silently, she added, *Nor was it ever a marriage in that way. But no one must know, Hugo said so himself.* Aloud she forced herself to add, "Had there been a child, I would have written you."

"Of course," Elizabeth told Drusilla soothingly. "You mustn't let my impertinent son upset you. We know very well that you would have written to tell us and that we would have welcomed the child eagerly as one more reminder of poor, dear Hugo. But that was not to be," she said with a sigh as she dabbed at her eyes with a bit of lacy handkerchief.

Drusilla leaned farther back into the shadows herself before she asked, "Why did Hugo never marry? Until he met me, of course."

Elizabeth hesitated, but Julian answered forthrightly, "Because he was a rather selfish fellow who liked his comfort. He was forever telling us that he would not have his life put all to sixes and sevens by some interfering female."

"Julian!" his mother said severely. "What will Drusilla think of you?"

"I will think that he knew a very different Hugo than I did," she said with a sad smile. "The very last word I should have used with respect to Hugo was 'selfish.' Indeed, he was all that was kind and generous when I knew him."

Julian snorted. "He would have been—to you. All right, Mother, I shall hold my tongue. But Aunt Drusilla did ask a question and I was only quoting Uncle Hugo's reply."

"Oh, as to that," Drusilla said, "I can hear Hugo saying those very words. He liked to disparage himself as being harsh and unfeeling, but then he would turn around and offer kindness to someone who was nearby and needed it."

"Anyone except his family," Julian muttered.

He spoke so softly, however, that Drusilla could not be sure she had heard aright. Nevertheless she was glad, as they all were, when the carriage drew to a halt outside the Lawford town house.

In the lighted foyer Elizabeth looked at her young guest closely. "You *are* tired," she said with concern.

"It's off to bed with you, right this moment. Time enough tomorrow for a comfortable coze about tonight."

Gratefully Drusilla took the candle Julian held out to her, and turned to go up the stairs. In her room Annie, her maid, waited to help her out of her gown. Annie was built in the same tall, slender proportions as her mistress, and Drusilla often found herself wondering how Annie must feel looking at the dresses that she would never wear but that would, nevertheless, have fit her perfectly. Did she wish she could change places with Drusilla?

"Well," Annie demanded as she hung up the wine-colored confection, "were you the prettiest lady there, as I told you you would be?"

Drusilla laughed. "No, and I should not have said it if I had been. But I will allow that the gentlemen did not appear to precisely find me an antidote."

Annie nodded knowingly. "We'd best get you to bed, then, for the gentlemen will come calling tomorrow." She paused, then added, offhandedly, "Was his lordship there, ma'am?"

Drusilla was amused. "Which lordship?" she asked. "There were quite a few."

"Lord Pensley, ma'am," Annie replied, putting the last of Drusilla's things away.

"Why should you ask that?"

Annie sighed in mock exasperation. "As if I didn't know, ma'am, that he's been in your thoughts all day! Asking me if I'd heard whether his lordship planned to remove to London for the Season. Asking if I knew whether his lordship was acquainted with the Earl of Ormsby."

Drusilla colored. Turning to her dressing table and beginning to brush out her hair, she said as lightly as she was able, "Yes, Lord Pensley did come. So did Mrs. Fletcher."

"And I'll make no doubt you outshone her, as you always will," Annie said stoutly.

Drusilla turned to meet her maid's eyes directly. "You are a treasure, Annie," she said ruefully, "and I don't know how I was so fortunate to find you!"

Annie beamed with pleasure but scoffed in a severe tone of voice, "Stuff and nonsense! If you hadn't found me, you would have found someone just as good. I'm the one who's fortunate. Having you take me. It's been a good year, it has, and I'm grateful you hired me when you did."

"Ah, but I should think you would tax me with luring you away from London and burying you in the countryside," Drusilla rallied her.

"Not a bit of it!" Annie snorted. "I won't say as how I dislike London, for there's no denying that there's always a bit of excitement to be had here. But at my age one begins to enjoy the peace and quiet of the countryside."

"And a certain coachman?" Drusilla hazarded.

"Will that be all, Mrs. Lawford?" Annie asked with a sniff that said she would answer no such impertinent questions.

Drusilla knew the twinkle in her maid's eyes too well to be deceived, however, and she said, "Yes, that will be all. But you are not so old, scarcely above thirty, Annie, to be talking fustian about peace and quiet!"

For a brief moment the two women grinned at each other and then Annie was once more the proper lady's maid, dropping a curtsy and withdrawing for the night.

Alone Drusilla slowly climbed into the bed and

drew the covers over her. It was several minutes,
however, before she blew out the candle—several
minutes devoted to the contemplation of a certain
face and the smile she had scarcely expected to see.
Perhaps that was why, in spite of her fatigue, it was
some time before she fell asleep.

7

Drusilla Lawford found the next several days a round of *ton*ish parties and visits as well as drives about the city with the gentlemen who had pledged themselves to her amusement. Elizabeth Lawford professed herself all delight and even Julian was heard to remark over breakfast, late one morning, that it was very fortunate for him. As Drusilla looked at him with some surprise, he explained, his eyes twinkling, "Now my mother shan't expect me to always be squiring you about. Not that I should dislike it, but . . ."

"But you are rather more fond of your clubs and friends and such," Drusilla concluded for him.

Julian managed to execute a half-bow while still seated. "Precisely, though it is not civil of me to say so."

"But you didn't," Drusilla parried, "I said it for you."

Elizabeth threw up her hands in mock dismay, but she too laughed. "Children!" she said with a speaking look at Drusilla and Julian. "For I do think of you as the daughter I never had," she explained to Drusilla. "Somehow I cannot think of you as my sister-in-law. You are far too young and pretty for that!"

"You are kind to say so," Drusilla replied, coloring. "And I am fortunate in having found such good friends."

"Pish and tosh," Julian said, waving a careless hand. "We are very selfish, you see. It does our credit no end of good for everyone to see that we have as our houseguest such a reigning belle of the *ton*."

Drusilla shook her head in mock warning. "I shall not be a reigning belle for long. I have had it upon excellent authority that a certain Miss Cecelia Longworth arrives in London today and no male shall be able to resist her charms."

Julian threw up his hands and said, "You see? You have confirmed my opinion out of your own mouth. What other beautiful young woman would take so quickly to the Season that she hears the *on-dits* of the *ton* even before I do?" He leaned forward and said confidingly, "As for Miss Longworth, however, *I* have it upon excellent authority that she cannot hold a candle to you."

"Mere prejudice," Drusilla retorted swiftly. "You wish to maintain your reputation as my host and therefore will spread any calumny about poor Miss Longworth. I shall have to warn her about your dastardly motives."

Julian laughed but Elizabeth said thoughtfully, "It might be an excellent notion, Julian, if you did make Miss Longworth's acquaintance. You are, after all, five-and-twenty, and it is time you began looking about for a wife."

"A wife?" Julian was affronted. "I have some time, Mother, before I need worry about that. And if it were time, I should certainly look first at Aunt Drusilla. But you must realize that for now I am quite content to spend my time with my friends and leave the other gentlemen of the *ton* to do the pretty to the ladies.''

More than one fellow might have been surprised to hear Julian's words. He had not, it was true, ever attached himself to any of the young ladies of the *ton* who made their come-out each year. On the other hand, he was rumored to be excessively fond of those women who formed the demimonde of London. Or had been. Indeed, though his mother and uncle had worked quickly to hush up the scandal, it was due to one of these fair cyprians that Julian had been sent down from Cambridge some years before. Still, of late there had been disturbing rumors that Julian Lawford's tastes were somewhat eccentric, as the more discreet phrased it. Others were more blunt. At any rate, there was a vast difference between keeping a high flyer of any sort and looking about for a wife, and until this year no one would have accused Julian of the latter.

But already there were some tattleboxes who had noted that Julian Lawford was being surprisingly attentive to his mother's houseguest. Indeed, more than one jealous fellow had been heard to complain that Julian was taking unfair advantage of his position to place himself upon comfortable terms with the fair widow. After all, one never saw her look at him with that freezing expression she bestowed on those gentlemen who pressed their attentions too closely.

As for Drusilla, she was unaware of anything except that she was having the most delightful time of her life. Even the weather conspired to add to her happiness, for the cold spell had broken and sunshine warmed the city.

"Shall you be going out today?" Elizabeth asked Julian a trifle anxiously.

"Well, yes, I meant to go to Manton's for some shooting practice. Why?" Julian asked with a frown.

Elizabeth fluttered her hands. "It is of no great moment, save that I had intended to visit a dear friend of mine, Lady Welton, and I cannot think but that it would be a bore for Drusilla to come with me."

"And you thought I might entertain her?" Julian hazarded with a smile.

Drusilla intervened a trifle impatiently. "I am no child who must always be amused, Elizabeth. There is no need for me to accompany you or for Julian to alter his plans in the slightest."

"Well, but to leave you unchaperoned," Elizabeth protested. "I cannot like it, for it's no use pretending the gentlemen will not come to call."

"I am a respectable widow and not a green girl," Drusilla replied firmly. "I scarcely think I need be attended so closely as that. But if you are worried, perhaps it will reassure you if I tell you that I had intended to go out for a walk, on my own, in any event."

"On your own?" Elizabeth asked nervously.

"With a footman or maid in attendance, of course," Julian put in smoothly with a wink to Drusilla.

She did not protest this high-handedness but instead agreed, "I promise I shall be all propriety."

"Very well," her hostess said with a sigh. "I cannot deny that you have eased my mind considerably.

Well, if that's settled, then I shall go upstairs and get my things. Lady Welton will be waiting for me."

"And I," said Julian, rising, "am off to Manton's. Enjoy your walk, Aunt Drusilla."

"I shall," she murmured.

Sometime later, dressed in a warm and serviceable, rather than entirely fashionable gown of green merino, Drusilla donned her warmest pelisse trimmed with fur and gloves to match. Upon her head sat her warmest bonnet, for although the sun might have come out, Drusilla still felt the chill far too easily. The not uncommon result, she thought wryly, of six years spent in the climate of India.

A trifle guiltily she left the house alone. It was no part of her desire to distress Elizabeth, but she simply could not bear to be burdened with a footman or maid to dog her footsteps. With a brisk pace she set off for the nearest park.

As she turned into the gates, it was quite evident to Drusilla that she was not the only resident of London to have taken the notion of a visit to the park. She was the only one, however, who could lay claim to being a fashionable member of the *ton*. Among the youngsters playing there were no doubt some who would one day grace the rooms of Almack's, but for now they were more at ease playing ball while their governesses enjoyed a comfortable coze together. Well, that was just as well, Drusilla told herself with a sigh of relief. Even Elizabeth could not accuse her of being indiscreet when it was impossible that she would meet anyone who knew her.

All at once, as Drusilla trod down one of the paths, two muddy figures hurtled themselves toward her.

Instinctively she jumped back and just avoided being knocked over. "Beg pardon, ma'am," one of the boys called out, not in the least slowing his attack upon the other.

"Aye, beg pardon," the other seconded, managing to land a punch.

Ordinarily Drusilla Lawford would have had the sense not to intervene. She had, after all, been raised with several brothers. But under the circumstances she could not simply walk away. "Alfred Pensley?" she demanded loudly. "Is that you?"

Astonished, both boys stopped fighting and looked at her. Sheepishly, the smaller of the two scuffed a toe in the gravel of the path and said, "You won't tell on me, will you?"

The other snorted contemptuously and Drusilla fixed him with a stern eye. "Tell on whom? This young ruffian who cannot refrain from bullying boys smaller than himself?"

"It weren't like that," the boy protested hotly.

"Alfred?" Drusilla asked.

Young Pensley looked down at his feet. "No, it wasn't," he conceded reluctantly. "I started it."

"But why?" Drusilla demanded.

The two boys looked at each other and it was quite evident to Drusilla that an agreement was reached, for neither would answer her question. "I just did," Freddie replied stoutly.

"Oh, very well," she said, conceding defeat. "Where is your, er, tutor, Mr. Fargraves?"

"At home with a head cold," Freddie answered with a grin. "That's why I'm out on my own—there's no one to take charge of me just now."

"I see," Drusilla said grimly. "Well, I think it might be best if I escorted you home, right now."

"Why? So you can tell on me?" Freddie demanded.

"So that you can be cleaned up and have something cold put upon your eye," she replied ruthlessly. "I haven't the slightest interest in telling on you, but I would like to see that someone makes sure you haven't been seriously hurt."

At this the other boy intervened impatiently. "We were just fighting, ma'am. It's not as if I'd drawn his cork, or anything."

"No, he drew yours," Drusilla observed dryly, and had the satisfaction of seeing the boy hastily wipe his bloody nose with his sleeve. "But you have given him a shiner. So come along, Freddie, and tell me where your father lives."

Pensley regarded Drusilla with a calculating look. After a moment he said, "I won't. Tell you where he lives, I mean."

"And why not?" she asked steadily.

"Because everyone will make a fuss," he replied just as steadily. "But I will let you take me to your house and clean me up," he added generously.

"Oh, you will, will you?" Drusilla said sharply. "I begin to think you are very much like your father, after all. Very well, I shall take you home with me on condition that you allow me to send word to your father." Freddie started to protest and she went on sternly, "Or I call the watch and have them return both of you boys home. I will not have everyone worrying where you are, Freddie." Coaxingly she added, "Come, Freddie, we shall have you quite presentable before anyone can arrive to take you home."

"All right," he said reluctantly, and started down the path ahead of her.

Drusilla followed, pausing only to tell the other

boy, "I should try to get cleaned up as well, before my mother saw me, if I were you."

He merely grinned at her and said, "Don't worry, I shall."

Then she started after Freddie. To her surprise, once they reached the gate of the park, he immediately started off in the right direction. "How do you know where I live?" she asked him, a puzzled look upon her face.

Freddie shrugged. "Oh, Father drove past the other day. He said you were staying there. Mrs. Fletcher said the house looked a bit small, but *I* didn't think so."

Lost in her own thoughts, Drusilla did not reply. Instead, she concentrated on trying to think of just what story she was going to tell Elizabeth and her servants.

As it turned out, she need not have worried. Burrows took one look at Freddie and then said, in an expressionless voice, "I shall send up some hot water, Mrs. Lawford, and some spare clothes for the boy. I believe we've a lad about the same size employed in the kitchen."

"Thank you," Drusilla said coolly. "I should like someone to take charge of young Pensley while I write his lordship a brief note. As you say, he needs a bath, clean clothes, and attention to his eye. And someone must take 'round the note straightaway I have finished it."

"Very good, ma'am," Burrows said in the same expressionless manner. "This way, Master Pensley."

Freddie grinned at Drusilla and said, "I knew you were a great gun."

"That's all very well, but upstairs with you," she

told him with an answering grin that belied the
sternness of her voice.

Then she went into the bookroom to compose a
note to the boy's father.

8

Lord Pensley had just sat down to a breakfast of eggs and beef when a footman brought him a note. He regarded the fellow with surprise but said nothing as he opened the missive.

"Something important?" asked his sister Lady Ratherby, who had arrived the day before for, as she put it, a brief shopping expedition and respite from motherhood.

Pensley frowned and replied, "Perhaps. Freddie appears to have renewed his acquaintance with Hugo Lawford's widow. I told you about her, Cordelia. Well, she has written me a note to reassure me that he has not simply disappeared but is with her."

Cordelia, who was as intelligent as her brother and as pretty as he was handsome, raised her eyebrows as she asked, "But oughtn't the boy to be with his tutor? I thought you brought the fellow to London expressly so that Freddie would not fall behind in his studies or into excessive mischief."

"That is precisely the question I should like to ask," Richard replied grimly. Turning to the footman, he added, "Please ask Mr. Fargraves to step into the breakfast room."

The footman coughed discreetly and said, "Well,

as to that, m'lord, Mr. Fargraves is suffering from a terrible bad head cold and hasn't left his bed since yesterday."

"Since yesterday," Pensley exclaimed. "Why wasn't I told?"

The footman coughed again. "Well, you were quite busy, m'lord, and we all thought Master Pensley would tell you."

"I see," Richard said grimly. "No doubt he forgot. Very well, thank you, James. And what the devil are you laughing about, Cordelia?"

"Freddie," she answered frankly. "He greeted me quite warmly yesterday and talked all about his studies but never gave me the least hint his tutor was taken to his bed."

"You may find it amusing, but I do not," Richard said, fixing his sister with a stern gaze. "He ought not to have done it."

"Of course not," Cordelia agreed, "but what boy would resist the chance to go off on his own? You could not, did not, the time Mama and Papa brought you to London when Mattie was making her come-out. I distinctly remember an occasion when the entire household was thrown into sixes and sevens because you were nowhere to be found."

A reluctant grin surfaced on Pensley's face, and his sister went on, speaking carelessly, "Indeed, I don't know what has made you take on such a Friday face over a harmless piece of boyishness. You never were a Puritan before, Richard. Come, the boy is safe, apparently, and if you are honest, you will tell me that you would be far more disappointed if Freddie lacked the resolution to get up to mischief."

"True," Pensley conceded, "though I might wish

he had not chosen to thrust himself on Mrs.
Lawford."

"Why not?" Cordelia asked, taking a bite of eggs.

"Why not?" Richard echoed blankly.

"Yes, why not?" Cordelia repeated calmly. "I have
it on excellent authority—Freddie's—that Mrs.
Lawford is a 'great gun, bang up to the mark, and the
best of fellows.' Which I collect to mean that she
answers all his questions with astonishing patience."

Irritably Richard replied, "Yes, well, that is just
the trouble. I don't want him trying her patience too
far."

"I see," Cordelia said, dabbing at her lips
delicately with her napkin. "You know, I think I shall
come with you when you go to retrieve the boy."

"But there is no need," Richard protested.

As he watched her, Cordelia rose and said sweetly,
"Yes, I know, but my curiosity has been awakened by
this woman who can arouse such devotion in Freddie
and such confusion in you. I shall be ready in a
quarter of an hour."

"But . . . but your shopping," Richard tried again.

Cordelia waved a careless hand. "There is plenty of
time for that. Giles told me to enjoy my trip to
London and not to hurry back until I was ready."

"How convenient," Richard said dryly.

"You know very well Giles cannot abide London,"
Cordelia said indulgently, "but he is kind enough to
know that I love the Season and he really does want
me to be happy."

Pensley gave in to the inevitable. "Very well, you
may go with me. But I shall leave in forty minutes,
not fifteen."

"Why?" Cordelia asked.

"I wish to change my coat," he replied coolly.

Cordelia stared at her brother with dancing eyes. "Indeed? I see nothing wrong with this one, save that it is not quite as new as some. Now I wonder why you wish to impress Hugo Lawford's widow?"

"Cordelia . . ." he said in a dangerously quiet voice.

"Very well, not another word," she said, and fled, laughing.

Unperturbed, Pensley continued his breakfast.

A little over an hour later Lord Pensley and his sister stood on the steps of the Lawford town house. An impassive Burrows took their wraps and led them into the drawing room. For a moment Richard stood stunned by the sight that met his eyes. Mrs. Lawford was down on the floor playing spillikins with Freddie.

But then the pair spotted their guests and hastily rose to their feet. It was impossible to tell, Richard thought with private amusement, which of them appeared more embarrassed. Aloud he said, coolly, "Hallo, Freddie. Good morning, Mrs. Lawford. May I present my sister Lady Ratherby?"

The two ladies exchanged greetings, then Richard once more eyed his son and said, "Am I mistaken, Freddie, or are those clothes a new addition to your wardrobe?"

Freddie looked at Drusilla, who stepped bravely into the breach. With creditable calm she replied, "The clothes belong to the houseboy who works in the kitchen. Reprehensible of us, no doubt, to dress him so, but there was a slight accident to Freddie's clothes that necessitated the change. His own will be ready shortly."

Moving closer to her nephew, Cordelia observed dryly, "No doubt the same, er, accident accounts for

the delightful shiner Freddie is beginning to sport?"
Drusilla looked stricken but Cordelia went on in a
friendly way, "Don't be alarmed, Mrs. Lawford. As
the mother of several boys and the sister of one, I
have seen a great many shiners in my time, and *I* do
not find them the least alarming, though I should like
to know how Freddie acquired this one."

A sigh of relief escaped from Drusilla. "I, too, have
brothers," she said, and a warm look passed between
the two ladies. "Which is one reason, perhaps, why I
did not think to refine too much upon the matter of
Freddie's, er, shiner. As for how he got it, I gather he
was defending his honor."

"Indeed?" Richard's entire face expressed disbelief.

Drusilla met his eyes coolly. "I think so," she said.
"I cannot think of any other reason he would refuse
to tell me the cause for his fight."

"I see," Richard said. "And where was this fight?"

Exasperated, Freddie decided to answer for himself. "In the park. And Drusilla is quite right: it was
an affair of honor."

With great effort Pensley ignored his sister's
gurgle of laughter. Fixing his son with a dis-
approving stare, he asked quietly, "Drusilla?"

Freddie colored. "M-Mrs. Lawford, I mean," he
stammered.

Richard turned to her and said, with a slight bow,
"My apologies, Mrs. Lawford. This rapscallion seems
unable to leave you in peace."

He was not entirely surprised when she replied,
"But I don't want him to!" She paused, then added
severely, "I know it is not considered *comme-il-faut*,
here in London, for Freddie to visit me, but there is

no harm in the boy, and I like him. As for when I am at Lawford Manor, surely you can have no objection to him visiting me there?"

"Unless you marry," Richard found himself saying. "Your husband might not be as welcoming of Freddie as you are."

"My husband?" Drusilla looked at Pensley in bewilderment.

Cordelia's laugh intruded. "I collect my brother to mean, Mrs. Lawford, that he cannot conceive of why you are in London for the Season unless you intend to renounce the state of widowhood."

"Particularly as you have so quickly abandoned mourning," Richard could not resist pointing out.

Through gritted teeth Drusilla answered, "I came to visit my sister-in-law, who was kind enough to invite me. And it was she who persuaded me that Hugo would not have wanted me to grieve for him forever."

"Mrs. Lawford or her son, Julian?" Lady Ratherby could not resist asking. "Unless he has greatly changed, young Lawford is a very handsome gentleman."

Drusilla laughed. "So he is. And I'll not deny that he has been as eager as his mother to see me go out and about and enjoy myself."

Lord Pensley frowned. "I should not," he said carefully, "rely too greatly upon Julian Lawford's advice, Mrs. Lawford."

"Why not?" Drusilla asked, puzzled. "Do you fault it?"

"Not in this case," Richard conceded with alacrity. "It is merely that the boy is known as something of a scoundrel. Heedless at the least, possibly far worse."

"Unfair," Drusilla cried. "I should have thought that you were above such nonsense as listening to gossip."

Pensley regarded her steadily for a long moment. "You champion him readily," he said at last.

"And why not?" Drusilla demanded. "He has shown me nothing but kindness, and I have a fondness for Julian Lawford."

Troubled, Richard said, "Just so. But I must warn you, Mrs. Lawford, that he is one person I would never give my permission for you to marry."

"Marry?" Drusilla gasped. "You must have windmills in your head, for I have hinted no such thing." Then, goaded, she said, "If you think that Julian is a heedless ne'er-do-well, then I can only say that you must be unacquainted with him, for I have never met a kinder gentleman nor one more eager to see to my comfort or his mother's."

For a moment Pensley stood frozen looking at her, then he bowed and said impassively, "Please recollect, Mrs. Lawford, that I am a man of my word. If you marry Julian Lawford before your twenty-fifth birthday, you forfeit Hugo's fortune."

"Richard," Cordelia began to protest, "don't you think you go too far?"

"Much too far," a lazy voice agreed from the door of the drawing room.

"Julian!" Drusilla cried out.

Young Lawford strolled coolly forward. "Lord Pensley. Lady Ratherby, I collect? Good day to you. And this boy?"

"My son," Richard said tersely.

"I see." Julian nodded. "May I ask what this is all about? And what gives you the right, or wish, to meddle in my Aunt Drusilla's affairs, Lord Pensley?"

Richard had regained his composure and he spoke briefly and without emotion. "Until her twenty-fifth birthday, I am in charge of Mrs. Lawford's inheritance. By the terms of Hugo Lawford's will, if she marries without my permission during the next five years, she loses that inheritance."

Julian paled. "And where does it go?" he asked. "Into your pockets, I suppose?"

Pensley shook his head. "That is unworthy of you, Lawford. The money goes neither into my pocket, nor hers, nor, I might add, yours. That is all Nicholson will tell me."

"I see," Julian said. Recovering, he turned to Drusilla and took her hand in his. "Shall I ask this impertinent fellow to leave?" he said. "Lord Pensley's suspicions, however nonsensical, cannot help but distress you."

"You need not ask us to leave," Pensley said coolly. "Freddie, come along. I shall send someone 'round for your clothes later and return these at the same time. Cordelia?"

With warm sympathy in her voice, Lady Ratherby addressed Drusilla. "I am so glad to have met you, Mrs. Lawford, and I can well see why Hugo persuaded himself to abandon bachelorhood. I hope we shall meet again while I am in London."

Even Freddie came up beside her and said, "I'm sorry to have caused such a bother."

Drusilla bent down and gave him a hug, saying warmly, "Nonsense! None of this is your fault and I am very glad I ran into you in the park."

"Freddie," Pensley said impatiently, "it is time to go."

Drusilla watched them leave and then turned, coloring deeply, to her nephew. "I'm sorry, Julian," she said. "I cannot understand how Lord Pensley came to have such a foolish notion. And I am sorry that his dislike of me has carried over so that he now dislikes you as well."

Once more Julian possessed himself of her hand as he said, in the kindest voice imaginable, "Nonsense! As you said to young Pensley, none of this is your fault. I have long thought Lord Pensley to be a trifle touched in the upperworks and I can only conclude myself to have been right. What possessed Uncle Hugo to name him your guardian is beyond me."

There was no time for Drusilla to answer, however, for at that moment Elizabeth bustled in, full of curiosity as to why Lord Pensley and his son and his sister had just departed her doorstep.

9

Drusilla spent much time in the next few days wondering about the Pensleys. What a pity it was so frowned upon for Freddie to call upon her. Meanwhile, Elizabeth and Julian had been most understanding, never once referring to that dreadful interview with Freddie's father. Instead, they took her about, introducing her to all their friends and even arranging for a trip to the theater when Drusilla expressed a desire to see Edmund Kean perform.

"You should have seen him in his first season," Elizabeth told her young guest with a sigh over supper the day they were to go. "He is still marvelous, of course, but that year everyone went to the theater and he could not go anywhere without people stopping to stare."

"Well, I, for one, can scarcely understand why," Julian said carelessly, "for he reminds me of nothing so much as a trained monkey. He is surely no handsomer than one."

Drusilla started to protest until she saw the twinkle in his eyes. "Now you are roasting me," she told him severely, "and that is scarcely kind of you."

He bowed and said, "*Mea culpa*, but I am taking you, so surely that is penance enough?"

In answer Drusilla merely turned her head and

spoke to Elizabeth about another matter. Again, Julian laughed.

In spite of all his teasing, Julian was a most attentive fellow as he threaded his way through the theater lobby with his mother and Drusilla later that evening. Drusilla would have stopped to stare had they not been so late. Indeed, they scarcely had time to take their seats in the Lawford box before the curtain rose and then all eyes were on the stage.

All eyes, perhaps, save those of Lord Pensley. It was not that he disdained Kean. Indeed, he was a great admirer of the fellow. It was simply that a fair figure dressed in a gown of blue silk had caught his eye. Richard watched, a twist of anger to his lips, as Julian Lawford pointed out something on the stage to his companions.

It was at this point that Pensley's two companions noticed that something was amiss. Cordelia followed the direction of her brother's gaze with a hint of a smile playing about her lips. Arabella Fletcher stiffened in her chair and leaned toward Pensley to ask him some question about the piece. *That* had the satisfactory effect of turning his attention back to her and to the stage.

Nevertheless Arabella could not feel at ease. Until she had seen Mrs. Lawford, she had been quite content with her own gown of green silk, for it was certainly as dashing as the one Drusilla had worn to the Earl of Ormsby's party. If Mrs. Lawford could give up mourning, then so too could she. But somehow that was not enough. Who could have guessed, she thought with lips pressed tightly together, that changing from black could have made such a difference in the mousy little widow?

Unaware of the consternation she was causing in Mrs. Fletcher's breast, Drusilla watched in rapt admiration the performance on stage. Indeed, when the curtain fell for intermission, she found she had to shake her head to return to the present.

". . . procure you a glass?" Julian was asking.

"Yes, I should like that," Drusilla replied hastily, hoping he would not think she had been rude.

Julian bowed and left, and it was Elizabeth's turn to startle her. "Someone is staring at you. Or rather three people are," she said calmly. "They've been doing it all through the play."

Drusilla looked in the direction her hostess indicated and colored. "Lord Pensley and his sister as well as Mrs. Fletcher," she said with a wretched feeling in her stomach.

"Indeed," Elizabeth agreed. "And how utterly extraordinary. I had thought so, but then it seemed impossible he and his guests could behave with such inexcusable boorishness. I was evidently mistaken."

Drusilla was too abashed to speak, but there was no need, for abruptly Elizabeth added, "Perhaps there is some sense to Julian's absurd notion, after all."

"What absurd notion?" Drusilla asked, puzzled.

Elizabeth waved a hand carelessly. "Oh, the foolish boy took it into his head that Pensley is warning you off other suitors because he wishes to marry you himself and get his hands on your fortune. But that is patent nonsense, for the Pensleys have never lacked for funds. At least, not that I am aware."

"Well, a less loverlike attitude I have never seen in

a gentleman," Drusilla said firmly, "nor a man less eager for a wife."

"Wishing to fix your interest, perhaps, by seeming unlike the other 'uns who flock about you," Elizabeth hazarded.

"My dear Elizabeth," Drusilla said quite firmly, "I like you very much, but I assure you that in this you are mistaken. Lord Pensley took me in the deepest dislike before we had even met."

"Ah, but since then?" Elizabeth asked wisely.

Drusilla looked away. Feeling a trifle breathless, she replied, "Oh, well, no doubt he dislikes me less, but that is all."

Elizabeth looked doubtful but did not press the matter further. Instead, she turned to wave to various friends scattered about in the other boxes.

Left to herself, Drusilla had to acknowledge that she had not told Elizabeth the precise truth. What Lord Pensley felt was beyond her comprehension. The first time he had met her he had said that she was not as awful as he had expected. Then, later, he had indeed seemed taken with her. But at Elizabeth's house the other day, it was as though something since had occurred to alter everything. Unfortunately Drusilla had not the slightest notion what had caused the change. She only knew that Lord Pensley had been angry and impatient and seemed to dislike her once more.

Why that should distress her so deeply Drusilla refused to consider. She was not such a fool, she told herself sternly, as to wear the willow for a man who did not even like her.

She was still deep in such thoughts when Julian returned and her attention was captured by his rapid

patter of amusing *on-dits* overheard, he claimed,
while waiting his turn to procure the refreshments.

"Gossiping with the wild blades from the pit, you
mean," his mother retorted affectionately. "But no
less the likely, for all that. So Lady Quimby is
increasing, is she? And her husband in his sickbed
these past six months and more. One wonders what
he will make of this fine news."

"Make of it?" a deep voice asked from behind
them. "Nothing, of course. If asked, he will merely
smile and thank the speaker for the compliment on
his virility."

"Lord Pensley," Julian and Elizabeth exclaimed
together.

Drusilla, silent, felt frozen in her chair, scarcely
able to meet Pensley's eyes and yet wanting to hear
his voice go on talking to her. With a start she heard
him say, "Mrs. Lawford, my sister Cordelia has
badgered me to come over here and ask you if you
will be so kind as to set aside the morning to go
shopping with her. An expedition which I have
already cried off from and which I will understand if
you also wish to avoid."

Somehow the easy amusement in his voice made it
possible for Drusilla to meet Pensley's eyes. To her
astonishment she heard herself say, "On the contrary, Lord Pensley, you must be aware that all
women delight in shopping and I should very much
like to accompany Lady Ratherby. So long as you are
not going along to dissuade us from spending our
shillings as we wish."

"Mrs. Lawford, you wound me," Pensley retorted
in affronted accents that would have done credit to
Kean. "To think that you imagine I would be so

foolish as to attempt to dissuade my sister from anything she wished to do! Besides, it is not the shillings that concern me, it is the pounds. Or they would be, if it were my money and not Lord Ratherby's she is spending."

Drusilla's eyes twinkled as she said demurely, "It was not Lady Ratherby I was thinking of. As trustee of Hugo's estate I am forever in a quake that you will lecture me on my extravagances."

With mock severity he replied, "My dear Mrs. Lawford, you know very well that you have not once, in the past year, contrived to outrun the piper, not once applied to Nicholson for extra funds."

"Ah, but that was before I came to London," Drusilla countered. "You can scarcely have expected me to dissipate my fortune in Cropthorne; I shouldn't think it would be possible."

At this point Julian intruded. With no attempt to hide his dislike of Lord Pensley he said, "The curtain is about to rise and you had best make haste back to your own box, m'lord."

Pensley bowed. "Very well. My sister will call for you at ten, if that is convenient, Mrs. Lawford."

"Most convenient," Drusilla assured him with a warm smile.

And he was gone.

Both Julian and his mother refrained from commenting upon the incident until they were in the carriage and headed home. Then Elizabeth said gently, "Do you think, my dear, that you are altogether wise to encourage that connection? With Lord Pensley's family?"

Drusilla smiled at her hostess reassuringly. "Why not? I like Lady Ratherby. She has none of the arrogance or rudeness her brother is capable of, but she does have the kindest of eyes. In any event, what am I to do? At home I am neighbor to Lord Pensley, and even here I must look to him or Nicholson for funds." She hesitated, then took a deep breath and went on frankly. "As yet, I do not contemplate remarriage, but the time may come when I will. I should prefer, then, to be upon civil terms, at least, with Lord Pensley. For if I am less than twenty-five years of age I must have his approval or forgo Hugo's inheritance entirely."

Again Drusilla paused. This time she spoke ruefully. "I do not deserve Hugo's kind of legacy, I know, but I have grown accustomed to it. I should dislike losing it merely because I am unable to keep upon level terms with someone."

Julian was the first to answer. "That is my Aunt Drusilla," he said approvingly. "An excellent, intelligent answer for everything! Well, I, for one, agree with you. After all, it is not as though you were encouraging *his* attentions. Go tomorrow and enjoy your expedition with Lady Ratherby. Perhaps she can even be persuaded to make Pensley see reason."

Elizabeth sighed. "You are both right and I am a foolish old woman. Go and buy yourself some pretty fripperies, Drusilla, and bring Lady Ratherby to tea afterward."

Overwhelmed, Drusilla found herself saying, "I cannot believe how fortunate I am to have such kind friends."

Gallantly Julian retorted, "We are the ones who are fortunate."

Between them, the three managed to keep up a lighthearted banter all the way home.

Arabella Fletcher, meanwhile, was returned home

seething with conjecture as to Pensley's visit to the Lawford box. It was a question to which she had not the slightest hint of an answer. Arabella Fletcher disliked not having answers.

As for Lady Ratherby, she was considerably surprised to be informed in the carriage, after they had left Arabella at her town house, that she was to go on a shopping expedition with Drusilla Lawford the next morning at ten o'clock. "Shopping?" she repeated incredulously.

"Well, you said you meant to go," Richard retorted coaxingly. "And you are forever telling me how much you dislike to go shopping alone and you will not take Arabella with you, so why not Mrs. Lawford? Didn't you say you liked her?"

"Why, yes, of course I do," Cordelia said indignantly. "But what will she think of such an odd invitation? And tendered so abruptly? It is the sort of thing one does with friends, not with someone one has just met."

"But don't you want to be her friend?" Richard continued coaxingly.

Cordelia fixed her brother with a firm stare and said, "I think you had best tell me just what this is about, Richard."

"What do you mean?" he asked innocently. She did not answer but rather continued to stare, and after a moment he shrugged. "Oh, very well. It is simply that as her guardian I feel a certain responsibility toward her, and as she will not talk with me, I hoped that she might with you so I should have an idea how she goes on here in London. I cannot be altogether easy in my mind as to her visit with Hugo's sister and nephew. I am too well aware of his opinion of that pair."

There was a long silence and Pensley found himself holding his breath. At last his sister said, "Oh, very well. I admit I should like to see Drusilla Lawford again and I have no objection to making sure she is happily situated where she is. But I shall not pry. She must confide in me herself if she so chooses." Cordelia paused, then added thoughtfully, "She would talk with you, you know, if you were not at such pains to set her back up. I cannot think why you do it, for you are quite capable of charming everyone else we know. Why have *you* taken her in such dislike?"

"I have not," he retorted with a frown.

Cordelia was thoughtful again and it was several moments later before she said, with a triumphant smile, "Well, if you do not dislike her, then the only answer is that you have conceived a *tendre* for her and don't know what to do about it."

"Don't be absurd," Pensley all but shouted at his sister.

Quite unperturbed, Cordelia continued to smile. As she leaned back against the cushions of the carriage, however, she said, "The only difficulty that I see, aside from your need to cease being so prickly with Drusilla Lawford, will be how to dispatch Arabella Fletcher from your side. She has somehow convinced herself that you are the one who will end her widowhood and soon half the *ton* will be convinced as well." Cordelia looked at her brother, who was glaring at her. "Very well," she said reluctantly, "not another word. But I shall go on that shopping expedition with Mrs. Lawford. Ten o'clock you told her? Good. And you may be very sure I shall take care to discover how she is enjoying her stay in

London. To satisfy my own curiosity, not yours," she warned him, contradicting what she had just said before.

But with that Lord Pensley was content. He knew his sister well.

10

At precisely ten-fifteen the next morning Drusilla stepped into the barouche Cordelia had brought around for their shopping expedition. She wore her blue velvet pelisse over a gown of sprigged muslin that Elizabeth had assured her was quite *comme-il-faut*. On her head was a flower-trimmed bonnet that framed her face charmingly.

Lady Ratherby greeted her and then said, a wave of her hand indicating the carriage, "A trifle old-fashioned, I know, but so very comfortable. I hope you do not mind. Richard says I shall become positively dowdy at this rate."

Drusilla gazed at her companion's excessively modish bonnet with its curling feather and her sable-trimmed golden-brown pelisse over a dress of rose-colored cambric. Dark curls escaped, as intended, from the bonnet to dance about Lady Ratherby's face when she laughed or shook her head. And the brown of the pelisse precisely matched her eyes. With a laugh Drusilla retorted frankly, "My dear Lady Ratherby, it is my fervent wish that in ten years I should be as dowdy."

"But what is this?" Lady Ratherby demanded in mock dismay. "You must call me Cordelia and I shall call you Drusilla. and you are far too kind, though I must say that Giles has never had reason to complain of how I look."

"Giles?" Drusilla asked hesitantly.

"My husband," Cordelia replied with a laugh. "You would like him and he you, for he is forever telling me that a stint of time in some backwater place such as India would cure me of my inflated notions of my own consequence."

"Now you are roasting me," Drusilla said severely, "for I cannot imagine anyone less puffed up in their own conceit."

"Well, perhaps Giles is roasting me," Cordelia answered good-naturedly. "No doubt I give him cause."

"Is Lord Ratherby here in London with you?" Drusilla asked.

Cordelia shook her head. "No, he abhors London. Or so he says. But Giles is the kindest fellow imaginable and insists I come to visit Richard every time I start to grow restless in the countryside." Cordelia paused and her voice became serious as she added, "You may think me a shatterbrain, but I am not. I am all too aware of how fortunate Giles and I have been in our marriage. Perhaps that is why I hope Richard may find similar happiness. And *not* with Mrs. Fletcher."

For several moments Drusilla sat stunned. At last she ventured, "Do you . . . do you think you ought to speak to me about Lord Pensley's affairs? I cannot think it quite proper."

"Proper?" Cordelia snorted. "Of course it's not proper. And with anyone else I shouldn't dare. But you, you are different."

"How am I different?" Drusilla asked warily.

"You are different because," Cordelia retorted

swiftly, "you are one of the few females in London who is not constantly casting sheep eyes up at my brother. And because you are one of the few he does not altogether disdain and because Arabella Fletcher seems to have taken you in the greatest dislike and because I like you myself. All of which leads me to have a high opinion of your good sense. And I need to ask someone with good sense their opinion of Arabella Fletcher."

"Why?" Drusilla asked with curiosity. "No matter what my answer, I cannot see that there is anything you can or ought to do."

"Ah, but there is." Cordelia smiled to herself with satisfaction. "No, I shan't tell you, it is between Mrs. Fletcher and myself. I simply want your opinion of the woman."

Drusilla hesitated but at last she said, "I find I might almost like Arabella if she did not seem always to have half of her mind on other matters when she speaks to one. She is intelligent, and were her circumstances otherwise, I think she would be generous."

"What the devil do you mean by that?" Cordelia interrupted. "Fletcher left her very well-to-do."

"I-I don't know," Drusilla conceded slowly, "save that it seemed to me, when I met her, that she had had to fight, both for herself and for her child, and that much of herself was still on guard against further attacks." Drusilla stopped and shook her head briskly. "No doubt that is all nonsense," she said crisply. "I have only met her once and she was all that is kind to me."

"Kind?" Cordelia asked dryly. "How unlike Arabella. I should have said she had no care for anyone but herself. Are you certain she did not merely speak in kind accents while at the same time contriving to be abominably rude?"

"Perhaps," Drusilla conceded reluctantly.

"Did she speak of Lord Pensley?" Cordelia persisted. "You may as well tell me what she said, for I assure you that what I would otherwise imagine would be far worse."

"Very well," Drusilla said at last. "It is no more than you already know, I should think. Arabella made it clear she had come to see me to determine whether or not I was a rival with her for the . . . the attentions of your brother."

"And what did she conclude?" Cordelia asked with interest.

"That I was not the slightest danger to her desire to be Lady Pensley," Drusilla replied, unable to keep a trace of anger out of her voice.

At this Cordelia sat up abruptly and said, "Indeed? I should never have thought Arabella a featherwit. Certainly she did not seem to feel the same last night after Richard paid a visit to your theater box."

"Until we came to London neither she nor anyone else had seen me out of mourning," Drusilla replied dryly. "Nor at a time when I took more than a cursory interest in my clothes. That has changed since I arrived in London."

"Has it? I wonder why?" Cordelia said thoughtfully.

Drusilla laughed and became more animated than Cordelia had yet seen her. "That is no mystery. It is because of the kindness of Hugo's sister and nephew."

"Sister-in-law," Cordelia corrected.

"Well, yes, but she seems to have been as devoted

to Hugo as if she had been his real sister," Drusilla replied. "After such a difficult time—with Hugo's death and the death of my parents—it is so nice to have someone treat me with such kindness. It was Elizabeth who insisted I must not go on mourning Hugo forever, for he shouldn't have wanted that. And she who bullied me into purchasing some stylish gowns."

"And once she had, you discovered you did care about such things?" Cordelia hazarded shrewdly.

"Precisely," Drusilla said, pleased to be understood so easily. "And it is the first time in my life I have had the funds to freely indulge such an interest."

"I wonder what Elizabeth Lawford is about," Cordelia murmured quietly. "I have never known her to be kind before."

Drusilla bristled and would have protested such cavalier treatment of her hostess had the carriage not stopped just then. "Ah, here we are at the Pantheon Bazaar," Cordelia said with satisfaction. "Come along. Peters will meet us with the barouche in two hours. Meanwhile, let us see what bargains we may discover before then."

It was a huge place and Drusilla soon found herself caught up in the delightful task of choosing between gloves of the most delightful softness, silk stockings, fans of ivory and lace and painted parchment, reticules and handkerchiefs, bows and ribbons and slippers, as well as shawls and muslins and every other sort of goods to delight a lady's heart.

"I must buy this for Mrs. Lawford," Drusilla said as she held up a shawl of the finest Norwich silk. "Do you think she would like it?"

"She would be a ninny if she did not," Cordelia answered roundly. "But look here! Do you like this? Do you think it would suit you?"

Lady Ratherby held out a length of silvery gauze toward her young friend. Drusilla reached for it, then let her hand drop away. "No, I fear the color would suit you far better," she said regretfully.

Cordelia looked at the length of gauze again. "You are right, I suppose. Well, I shall take it and be glad to do so, I just had hoped to help you find something you would like."

A few minutes later Lady Ratherby had her wish. "The very thing!" she exclaimed.

This time Drusilla did not hesitate to agree. It was a piece of green Indian muslin shot through with gold threads, of a quality that might have been used to make a sari for an Indian woman of the highest caste. "It's beautiful," Drusilla whispered. Then a thought occurred to her and she added, "Do you think it wise, though? Won't it just remind everyone that I am come from six years in India?"

"Ah, so you've been snubbed because of that already," Cordelia said wisely. "Well, all the more reason to wear it. As a shawl, perhaps, but wear it you must! Always stand your ground, Drusilla, and speak of India as often as you can. If you cut and run, the *ton* will be after your blood, but if you stand up to them, they'll respect you all the more. Buy this and wear it," she concluded sternly.

Drusilla smiled. "Very well. Though I take leave to warn you that if it lands me in the briars, I shall tell everyone that it was you who bullied me into wearing it."

Both ladies laughed and good-naturedly continued

their shopping together. Gradually Drusilla found herself telling Lady Ratherby more than she had intended, both about her life in India and about her stay in London. The lightness with which she spoke of certain troubles in India and the difficulties and discomforts of the journey home endeared her to Cordelia. As did the patient way she answered all of Cordelia's questions.

"But why didn't you bring the *ayah* with you when you came back to London?" Lady Ratherby asked at one point.

"How could I?" Drusilla replied. "There were other servants as well whom I was fond of. But how could I bring any of them back to England when they have lived all of their lives in India? If the climate did not kill them, as Hugo told me it has done to many Indians brought back by otherwise kind people, they would be unbearably homesick for their own country, their own food, their own way of life. Should I have selfishly brought my *ayah* here when it would have meant tearing her away from her own family?"

Lady Ratherby sighed. "It is so hard to know what to do. Hugo and Richard are forever, were forever, telling me I must not go on picturing everyone in the world to be uncivilized and England the only place one could wish to be, but it is so very hard not to do so."

Drusilla smiled warmly at her friend. "And if you were to ask an Indian of the Brahmin caste, he would no doubt tell you the same about India. He would tell you that Indian civilization goes back farther than our own. Much farther. Don't you see? It is only natural for all of us to believe that our own way of life is the most comfortable and natural and civilized. I daresay someone from Africa or China would say the same thing."

"Well, what is the answer then?" Cordelia asked a trifle impatiently.

"There is none," Drusilla said gently. "No one way of life is perfect for everyone." She paused and Cordelia regarded her with uncertainty. "Why must there be an answer?" Drusilla demanded. "Only one best version of anything? Why can't there be room for all of us in this world?"

For a moment matters hung in the balance and then Cordelia laughed and said with a shrug, "I vow, you and Richard might be twins the way you agree on such matters. Well, it is all one to me, as I daresay I shall never be in the position of ever making any decisions concerning such things."

Out of deference to Lady Ratherby, Drusilla turned the talk to matters of fashion and of precisely what shade of glove one ought to wear with what gown.

It was quite some time later, after an exhausting round of shopping, that the two ladies found themselves once more in the barouche with no more shops to visit. "Well, where to now?" Cordelia asked.

"Elizabeth, Mrs. Lawford did suggest that I bring you back for tea," Drusilla offered.

"Richard did the same with me," Cordelia replied. She regarded her companion with unconcealed thoughtfulness and then said, "Richard's town house it shall be. I haven't the faintest notion whether or not we shall find him in, but his cook prepares the most marvelous cakes and such to go with the tea. We shall send 'round a note to Mrs. Lawford telling her where you are and next time we may go there."

Drusilla quashed the momentary sense of panic inside her breast and managed to say with creditable calm, "I should like that very much."

"Good, it's settled then. Peters," she called out to their driver, "we shall be going home now. Lord Pensley's town house. Then you may take Mrs. Lawford's packages and a note to the Lawfords' town house."

Peters, who had come around the side of the barouche to hear his orders, nodded. "Very well, m'lady."

11

Lord Pensley's London town house. "Do you like it?" Cordelia asked as a footman took their wraps. "I have always found it delightfully comfortable, which is why, perhaps, I have never badgered Giles to hire a house in London. This way I have an excuse to descend upon poor Richard whenever I come."

Without waiting for an answer, she led Drusilla to the drawing room, where she rang for the maid, who promised to bring around the tea trolley straightaway. The drawing room was, like much of the house, Cordelia told her, paneled in wood where it was not papered. The furniture was sufficiently old-fashioned to remind Drusilla of the vicarage her father had lived in until his voyage to India. The curtains were of lace, hung on either side of the casement with velvet, and let in what little sunlight there was in winter, though "We pull the heavier draperies closed in summer, when we are not usually here, to prevent the carpets from fading," Cordelia explained.

Just then the drawing-room door opened and Lord Pensley entered with a bow to the two ladies. Suddenly feeling a chill in her muslin dress, Drusilla moved closer to the fireplace. Cordelia noticed at once. "Are you cold?" she asked sympathetically. "I have just the thing. Wait here while I dash upstairs for a shawl for you. It will just take a moment."

Before Drusilla could protest, Cordelia was gone, leaving her alone with Pensley. In spite of his carefully brushed hair, neatly tied neckcloth, superbly fitted coat, and biscuit-colored trousers, he seemed as ill-at-ease as she. In a lazy voice he said, "Am I to felicitate you upon the success of your shopping expedition?"

"If you wish," Drusilla retorted indifferently.

"Well, if you need further funds you have only to tell me," he added gently.

Stung, Drusilla looked at him squarely and said, "There will be no need of that, I assure you. Contrary to your evident expectations, I am not a spendthrift and I expect to manage quite well within the limits of the funds available to me. And why should I not? It is a very generous allowance, indeed a larger amount than that with which my mother ran her entire household in India."

Pensley drew his eyebrows together in a puzzled frown. "Now, what the devil have I said to put you in such a temper?" he asked quietly. "I merely meant that it is easy to spend more than one intends. And why should you not? Your allowance is a very modest one, considering the amount of funds Hugo left you. Besides, expenses are rather higher here than in India," Pensley could not resist adding. "And you do have a household to maintain in the country."

The flush of anger in Drusilla died away and she was able to smile as she replied, "So I do, but you have arranged separate funds for that as well." She paused, then determinedly plunged on, "Will you tell me, Lord Pensley, why you have taken me in such dislike? Try as I will, I cannot guess the reason."

"Taken you in dislike?" Richard began, astonishment evident upon his face. "But I have not!"

"Then, why . . . the other day . . ." Drusilla found herself unable to put bluntly into words what she meant.

Abruptly Lord Pensley was himself once more. Not meeting her eyes, he said stiffly, "I am sorry, Mrs. Lawford, if my words the other day caused you distress, but I had no alternative other than to speak as I did. I cannot approve your marriage to Julian Lawford."

"There is no question of such a thing," Drusilla reminded him roundly, "but I wish you will tell me why you could not give your approval if there were. What reason could you have other than a dislike of me?"

"A dislike of young Julian," he retorted bluntly. In the next moment he crossed the several feet of room between them and took hold of Drusilla's arms. "Don't you see? It is because I do not hold you in dislike that I should forever bar a betrothal between you and Julian Lawford. Surely you have formed, by now, some notion of his character? Surely someone has told you of the mischief he has wreaked in the past?"

Reluctantly Drusilla pulled herself free and turned her back on Pensley, determined not to let him see the tumult his touch had aroused in her breast. "Mischief?" she asked a trifle breathlessly. "That is a reason to oppose a man? Character? I have seen only kindness and dignity and . . . and thoughtfulness in his behavior. Am I to disdain that as well?"

Pensley flung an oath at her and would have said more, but at that moment the door of the living room was thrown open and a boy dashed in, followed at a more sedate pace by Lady Ratherby.

"Drusilla," Freddie cried as he came up to her.

"I tried to restrain him," Cordelia said with a laugh as she placed the shawl she had fetched about Drusilla's shoulders, "but once he knew you were here, there was no stopping the boy."

"That's just as well," she retorted, "for I confess myself very glad to see *him*." To Alfred she added, "I see that your eye is quite healed."

He colored. "Yes, it is." Then, with painful correctness young Pensley went on, "I-I wish to apologize, Mrs. Lawford, for any distress or inconvenience I may have caused you that day. It was unpardonable of me and I shall never do so again."

Drusilla, however, had no patience with this speech. "Nonsense," she told him roundly. "I quite enjoyed seeing you again and so I said at the time. I should not have done so if I did not mean it."

"Yes, but Mrs. Fletcher said I had to apologize," Freddie explained earnestly. "She said that otherwise I would give you a disgust of me."

"I do not fail my friends so easily," Drusilla answered a trifle more gently. "Now come and join us for tea."

Reluctantly Pensley shook his young head. "I can't," he explained. "I'm well behind in my studies and must catch up. I just wanted to see you and apologize."

"Well, thank you, and I'm glad you did," Drusilla answered. She watched him take leave of his aunt and father, and when he was gone, she turned to Lord Pensley and said mildly, "His tutor seems to be a harsh taskmaster."

Cordelia laughed. "Mr. Fargraves? I should think Freddie drives him and not the other way 'round."

"Mr. Fargraves has a firm hand, certainly, but Cordelia is quite right in saying Freddie holds his own with the fellow," Pensley confirmed. "In fact, I should hazard that rather than going upstairs to study dusty books, Freddie has some more entertaining plan in hand. Perhaps a reenactment of some famous battle with his toy soldiers. Or some training in sports. Of late he has begun commenting that this footman or another would 'strip to advantage,' or 'shows great bottom,' or 'would soon have his cork drawn for he no doubt lacks science!' "

Drusilla laughed. "I should have known better than to envision Freddie a poor put-upon lad," she conceded reluctantly.

"Yes, so you should," Pensley agreed rudely as his sister poured out the tea. "Aside from Freddie's own abilities to protect himself from such treatment, you must have known I would not allow it."

Drusilla did not answer but took the cup Cordelia proffered. Lady Ratherby also gave a cup to Pensley, who had all but forgotten the existence of the tea tray. She had not missed the expression that had crossed her brother's face as he watched Drusilla with Freddie, and now she judged it time to intervene. "Wait until you have children of your own, Drusilla. You will see what a harsh road it is that we poor parents tread."

Over the rim of her cup, Drusilla's eyes met Cordelia's. "Harsh road?" she asked. "Perhaps. And yet I cannot help but think it an envious one. For all the trials my brothers and I brought to my parents, they never seemed to regret our existence. And when I look at Freddie, I find myself wanting such a child.

I should enjoy watching him grow and perhaps even helping him to grow."

"No doubt you would forsake all the fashionable frivolities of the *ton* to forever devote yourself to your children?" Pensley asked, disbelief patent in his voice.

Setting down her cup, Drusilla answered with a laugh. There was an edge to her voice, however, as she said, "Of course not! I do not believe in martyrdom. Nor have I ever believed that it is in the best interest of a child to so smother it with attention that the child never has a chance to find his or her own path to tread."

"And you think that I do not allow Freddie sufficient room to himself?" Pensley demanded.

"I never said such a thing," Drusilla protested. "It is you who challenged me."

For a moment their eyes met angrily and Cordelia hastily said, "This sparring is all very well, but I should much prefer to talk of other matters. Richard, you must tell Drusilla the latest *on-dit* you heard about his highness the Prince of Wales."

With as good grace as he could show, Pensley did as he was bid.

12

When Drusilla returned to the Lawford town house, she found Julian but not Elizabeth waiting for her. "Mother is upstairs," he explained. "A headache, I believe. She is stricken with them from time to time, and the only remedy is to lie down in a darkened room."

"Oh, dear," Drusilla said. "Ought I to go up to her, do you think?"

Julian stopped her by placing a hand gently on her arm. "No, please don't. What she needs just now is rest. Indeed, she told me that it was fortunate that you did not bring Lady Ratherby home for tea, after all, for Mother would have been a terrible hostess today." Seeing the look of worry that still creased his aunt's forehead, Julian said lightly, "From the number of packages that arrived a while ago I gather your shopping expedition was a success?"

Drusilla looked at him and smiled warmly. "Well, yes, I confess I did enjoy myself and perhaps did splurge a trifle. It is so nice not to have to count farthings for everything I wish to buy. It has never been that way for me before."

Julian took her hand. "No, until you married Hugo life had not been kind to you, had it?"

Gently Drusilla pulled her hand free. "I should not

say my life had been unhappy," she corrected him. "It is simply that a vicar's living is never a wealthy one, and there were a good many of us in the family."

"How glad I am you need never count farthings again," Julian told her.

"You are the one who is kind," she told him playfully, "and I am in a great deal of danger of being spoiled by it."

Once more he moved closer to her, "Spoiled? Impossible!" Drusilla retreated and Julian stopped, looked at her for a long moment, then said, "What is it, Aunt Drusilla? Has Lord Pensley warned you off me again?" She colored and he went on, "Telling tales, perhaps, about my schoolboy pranks?" Drusilla shook her head, feeling remarkably foolish. "Then, why do you seem to be running away from me?" he demanded.

"I don't know," she answered truthfully, "save that you have never acted before as though you regarded me as anything more than your odd aunt and now . . . now . . ."

"Now I might be just another one of your suitors?" Julian offered bitterly. She nodded and he went on, "You cannot guess how hard it has been for me to behave as just your nephew these past weeks. I think from the first day I saw you, here in this house, I felt this way. But I did not wish to act precipitously, nor did I wish to frighten you away, as I evidently am doing now. Believe me, I know you can do far better than to marry a nobody such as myself. And I truly had not meant to interfere with your happiness. But when Pensley spoke as he did the other day, I realized I felt too strongly for that. Is it too much to hope that you reciprocate my feelings?"

Drusilla turned her back on him to pace the room.

Julian waited patiently. At last she faced him. "I don't know," she said. "I like you, certainly, but more than that? I just don't know."

Julian lowered his head. "That is no more than I expected. You may believe, however, that I shall not embarrass you by speaking of this again unless I have reason to believe your sentiments have changed. Indeed, after Pensley's pronouncement the other day, I ought not to have spoken at all."

"Pensley's pronouncement has nothing to do with my sentiments," Drusilla said indignantly, "nor ought it to have anything to do with yours. If we were suited, we should be whether Lord Pensley agreed or not." She paused and her voice softened as she added, "I might wish we were, for you are a most estimable gentleman."

"Well," he said philosophically, "that is better than nothing, and I shall continue to hope—very quietly, of course—for something more. And now I shall cease discomforting you, for I have an engagement I cannot avoid and must be off. Good day, Aunt Drusilla."

"Good day, Julian," she replied softly as she watched him go.

At dinner Elizabeth was sufficiently recovered to be able to express an interest in everything Drusilla had seen and done that day. She seemed not in the least distressed that her guest had not brought Lady Ratherby back for tea, as she had requested, even repeating the comment Julian had made.

"I should have been a very poor hostess today," Elizabeth confessed. "These headaches do not come upon me often, but when they do, I cannot bear to do other than lie down."

Drusilla smiled. "My mother used to have them as

well, particularly in India. She went willingly with my father when he decided to uproot us all and go off to the far side of the world, but I cannot think it was a happy choice for her. Her health was never of the best and in India grew even worse."

"You poor dear," Elizabeth said sympathetically, "much of the work of running the household must have fallen upon your shoulders then."

"It did, but I can scarcely claim to have been put upon for that, since we had an excellent staff of servants who seemed to know what we wanted before we did ourselves," she answered with a laugh. "No, if I felt put upon it was because my father decided to start bible classes but of course he was too busy to run them himself."

"But as a clergyman . . ." Elizabeth began.

Drusilla shook her head. "You forget, before the Charter Act of 1813 Papa could not be a clergyman there. He was hired as a clerk in the East India Company, and as a clerk he was expected to function. And he did amazingly well, but in his spare time Papa also wanted to spread the word of God and so he decided *I* must teach bible school."

"The Company must have been very glad to have you there to civilize the savages," Elizabeth said righteously.

Again Drusilla shook her head. "There were a good many men—and I am not sure I disagree with them—who felt such proselytizing would do more harm than good. The uprising in '06 occurred because the sepoys were told they must trim their beards and wear different headdress and give up their caste marks," Drusilla explained, as she had done so often since returning to England.

"But what is wrong with that?" Elizabeth asked, as

had so many others. "It all sounds very reasonable to me. A matter of cleanliness and neatness. Order and discipline are very important in the military, surely you see that?"

"I see that and you see that and the East India Company saw that," Drusilla agreed grimly, "and that was precisely the problem. Because to the sepoys it wasn't a matter of order and discipline. To them it was a deliberate attempt on the part of the Company to make them break caste, become unclean, and therefore force them to convert to Christianity, for their fellow Hindus and Muslims would have had nothing to do with them had they followed orders."

"Good," Elizabeth said forthrightly. "The more Christians about the world, the better."

"No, it is not good," Drusilla all but shouted. "Why can't anyone see? However much we may wish to, we cannot force everyone in the world to be like ourselves, and we shall only create enemies and disaster if we try."

"But surely you are not opposed to sending out missionaries?" Elizabeth asked, a trifle shocked. "I am not particularly religious myself, but surely it is a good notion."

"When the missionaries are good people and bring good to the people they live among and work to convert by example and teaching without any resort to force, then yes," Drusilla agreed. "I am, after all, a vicar's daughter. But to try to shame others and tell them that they are inferior unless they believe precisely as we do, accomplishes nothing. Nothing useful, at any rate, for I have no doubt that such attempts will lead to further uprisings before we are through."

"Yes, well, perhaps," Elizabeth said doubtfully, her patience exhausted. "I cannot say. But I do wish we would change the subject and speak of something else—I cannot abide politics at the dinner table."

"All right," Drusilla agreed, her eyes dancing. "Ought I to buy peace, I wonder, by telling you now about the present I have bought you?"

"Present?" Elizabeth asked, her face lighting up.

"Yes. And I shall fetch it for you straightaway after dinner," Drusilla promised. "I should have brought it down with me, but I forgot," she confessed.

Her good humor restored, Elizabeth laughed. "Nonsense, you have much on your mind of late." She hesitated, then added, "Including my scapegrace son, no doubt." The startled look upon Drusilla's face confirmed Elizabeth's suspicions, and she went on hurriedly, "No, no, don't color up, my dear. You've nothing to be ashamed or embarrassed about. Julian told me he meant to speak to you today about his growing affections. I told him he ought not to impose upon a guest that way, particularly after Lord Pensley's words the other day."

"He . . . he was most circumspect," Drusilla said quietly, "and tried not to distress me."

"But you were distressed," Elizabeth guessed.

Drusilla nodded. "I like Julian," she hastened to add, "but I had not thought of him as a suitor and . . . and—"

"It all came as something of a shock to you," Elizabeth concluded for her. "Yes, I can well imagine it did, for Julian has been at some pains to conceal his feelings from you. Why he spoke today I cannot entirely understand, but if he promised, as I feel sure he did, that he will not speak of them again unless you wish him to, then you may rely on his promise. Julian always keeps his word." Elizabeth paused and regarded her guest shrewdly. "Does that make you feel better?" she asked.

"Much better," Drusilla agreed.

"Good! Now tell me about Lord Pensley's son. Has he recovered from his battle yet? Or didn't Lady Ratherby mention the boy?"

"She didn't need to," Drusilla answered with a laugh, "for Freddie made sure to come and tell me himself that he was all recovered. Or rather," she corrected herself, "he came downstairs to apologize for distressing me the other day, and I could see for myself that he had recovered entirely."

"A well-brought-up boy," Elizabeth said approvingly. "Someone has taught him proper manners."

"Yes, he is a good boy," Drusilla agreed warmly. "I cannot help hoping that if I ever marry again that I have a son like Freddie."

"Just so long as you do not have plans to wed Pensley himself," Elizabeth said dryly. "I understand he is spoken for."

Drusilla ought to have laughed at that and indeed she meant to, but somehow she found that more difficult than she had expected. Instead, she said lightly, "By the terms of Hugo's will, I had best wait a few years before I make any such plans. I should much dislike having to give Lord Pensley the satisfaction of denying his approval to my marriage."

"That man!" Elizabeth said with a shake of his head. "I cannot understand what possessed Hugo to write a will with such decidedly odd terms."

"He was very ill then," Drusilla said, defending her late husband, "even needing to dictate the will to the vicar. And yet I would swear he meant only kindness toward me. I suppose I seemed very young in his eyes."

"Well, never mind," Elizabeth said briskly. "A good man would take you even if Pensley did exercise his right of disapproval and stripped you of your inheritance. And as you say, perhaps it will be a few years before you want to marry anyway, and then it won't matter. But now, my dear, you'd best hurry upstairs and freshen up. Recollect that Farnham is to escort us to Lady Pontworth's ball." As the two ladies hastily rose, Elizabeth added, teasingly, "And don't forget to bring down my present!"

Drusilla laughed.

13

To Drusilla's surprise, Lord Pensley arrived early the next day and said, upon being announced, "I've come to take you out for a drive, Mrs. Lawford." In answer to the astonishment evident upon both her face and that of Elizabeth's, he added, "It has been drawn to my attention that I have been sadly neglecting my responsibilities as your guardian, Mrs. Lawford. My sister Lady Ratherby tells me I ought to repair that omission." Drusilla continued to stare at him and he said a trifle impatiently, "Come, come, Mrs. Lawford, I cannot have my horses standing about all day."

And so, fifteen minutes later, he was handing a rather bewildered Drusilla into his high-perch phaeton. Once they were both settled, he motioned for his groom to take up his perch behind them and then they were off for Hyde Park.

"Are you always so high-handed?" Drusilla asked as they pulled away from the curb.

He laughed. "Was I so very bad?"

"Yes," she retorted bluntly.

"I didn't mean to be. I simply decided it was time I took seriously my responsibilities as your guardian, and I didn't wish to give you a chance to set me down before I had even begun."

"So you said," Drusilla pointed out. "But I don't understand why. Surely your responsibilities extend only to financial matters? Oh, and approval of possible husbands, of course."

"Well, but that's it precisely," he said, as though astonished at her obtuseness. "I've got to protect you from fortune-hunters."

"Such as Julian Lawford?" Drusilla asked coldly.

"Oh, such as the Comte Verney, Stidwell, Hatherton, and whoever else may be hovering about hoping to get their hands on your inheritance," Richard replied airily.

"But they are scarcely as attentive as Farnham or Dunsworth or any of a number of other gentlemen who are possessed of perfectly adequate funds of their own," Drusilla said innocently.

"And do you favor any of them?" Pensley inquired. "I am asking purely in my advisory position," he added as an afterthought.

"Of course," Drusilla agreed equably. "Still, I'm afraid I must disappoint you," she lied. "Thus far my heart is untouched."

"What? Entirely?" Richard demanded, neatly threading his horses and high-perch phaeton through the park gates. "I should have thought that impossible. Is there no one whom you view with even mild approval?"

Drusilla shrugged, ruthlessly suppressing the tumult in her breast. "Oh, with mild approval, of course. But I thought you were asking me about potential husbands."

"Well, and so I was," Richard said.

Drusilla turned to face him and said with some asperity, "If you think that mild approval is a sufficient basis for marriage, I take leave to tell you that I do not. I shall require a far stronger feeling before I give my hand to anyone in marriage."

"Forgive me," Pensley said with no little irony. "I had not realized your marriage to Hugo Lawford was such a love match. Indeed, I had the impression it was something in the nature of an . . . an arrangement."

At this Drusilla colored deeply. With difficulty she said, "I . . . That was different."

"How so?" he asked ruthlessly.

"I had no choice," she threw back at him, starting to cry.

"No choice?" Richard demanded with even greater surprise. "Do you mean that he . . . that you . . ."

Tears gave way to a watery chuckle as Drusilla realized what Pensley was trying to say. "Good Lord, no," she replied. "That is not what I meant."

"I think perhaps you had better tell me about it, then," Richard said quietly. "You have told me enough to arouse my curiosity but scarcely enough to quiet my fears."

After a moment Drusilla said, "Very well. You know Hugo came back to India at the request of the East India Company. They wished him to travel about and gauge the mood of the country. Well, in the end he came to our remote station just in time to be part of the cholera epidemic. I don't know if you have ever seen cholera, but it is a horrible disease ravaging its victims so that their days are spent in the greatest of distress. My father died and then my mother. I was left alone, my brothers serving elsewhere in India and no one to take care of me." She interrupted herself to look at Pensley and say, "I have told you all this before."

"I find that I should like to hear it again," he answered grimly.

"Very well. It seems that before my father and mother died, Hugo gave his word to them that he would look after me. And he meant to. At that time he was not yet ill and it looked as though both of us would escape the cholera. Hugo meant to bring me back to England and put me in the care of some cousin or other. But then he contracted the cholera." Drusilla's voice faltered. "When it became clear he would not live, Hugo decided that the best way he could provide for me was by marriage. As his wife, he said, I could return to England with enough funds to live upon, and the right, by virtue of my widowhood, to make my own decisions. I thought him half-mad but he was determined and it seemed the only thing that would allow him to die in peace. But I swear I never knew he meant to leave me Lawford Manor or so much in funds. I thought it would be a small competence, something sufficient to keep me from starving. As I said, he married me out of pity or a sense of responsibility or some such thing."

Pensley sighed. "And I have told you before that I cannot credit Hugo with marrying you out of pity. I have my own suspicions as to why he did. But since he is dead, we cannot ask him to resolve the point." Then, abruptly, Richard asked, "Did he never explain to you why he wanted the bulk of his unentailed wealth to go to you and not to Julian?"

Drusilla shook her head. "No, and it has me in a puzzle, for I should have thought he would have given it to Julian to ensure the upkeep of the family seat. Unless, perhaps, he knew Julian to already be

flush with funds from his own father?" she
hazarded.

It was Richard's turn to shake his head. "No. To be
cruelly blunt, Julian Lawford and his mother have
long been considered to be scarcely one step ahead
of their creditors. Indeed, I should not be surprised
to learn he has borrowed upon the strength of his
expectations."

"But that is not what Elizabeth told me," Drusilla
protested. "They have given me no indication they
are not plump in the pocket or that they resent my
inheritance, as they must have done if they were as
desperate as you say."

Pensley gave a harsh laugh. "I don't expect you to
believe me, but I suspect they invited you to London
in hopes that you would marry Julian and then
everything would be kept in the family, nice and
tight."

"You are quite right, I don't believe it," Drusilla
said through clenched teeth, unable, however, to
forget Julian's behavior the day before.

To Drusilla's surprise Pensley placed a hand over
hers and in a gentle voice said, "Forgive me, I hope I
may be wrong. It was only a suspicion, and after all,
rumors may lie."

Intolerably aware of his touch, Drusilla forced herself to take a deep breath and say, "You are quite
right there. Gossip would have it that you are heartless and cruel, but I cannot allow it to be true."

"Are you so certain?" Richard asked cynically.

"Oh, yes," Drusilla said equably. "I remember, you
see, when my brother Johnny died. He had always
been my mother's favorite. And for a long time after
that she was much like you: never smiling or

laughing, turning herself inward and doing only what she must, cruel with words, and the need, at times, to hurt others as she had been hurt."

"I have not lost a child," Richard said frigidly.

"No, you have lost a wife, and that is far harder," Drusilla agreed. "She was, I understand, a gentle and lovely woman who gave of herself to those around her. Or so everyone told me when I was living next door to you. Can they all have been wrong?"

"No, they were not wrong," Pensley replied curtly.

"How can you help but still grieve for her, then?" Drusilla asked gently. "Oh, I know, I know! One is not supposed to speak of grief or other emotions. One is supposed to be well-bred and hide one's emotions behind a proper mask. But because you have been kind to me, I am speaking to you bluntly. If your wife was as I have said, then she would have wanted there to come a time when you ceased to grieve and began to live once more." And look at me, Drusilla wanted to cry out, but did not. Instead she went on, "No doubt you are afraid of being hurt again, but if you do not live, then you are wasting the legacy she left you and denying it to Freddie as well."

"Freddie?" Richard demanded.

"Yes, Freddie. For he cannot help but see how you have shut yourself off and find it hard not to do so himself," Drusilla told him bluntly. "I understand there was a time when you were ripe for any mischief, even driving the Bath Road and back at night for a wager. You were accounted the gayest of young men and the first one ready for adventure. Do you honestly believe your wife would prefer to see you as you are now?"

For a moment matters hung in the balance and even the groom at the back of the high-perch phaeton held his breath. At last, however, Pensley smiled wryly. "No wonder Hugo wanted you out of India," he said at last. "For he knew that otherwise the natives would have murdered you and the company would have had to avenge your death. Terrible for business!"

Drusilla laughed. "No, no, no. What he really wanted was revenge on everyone here."

"Oh, yes, I see, he has never forgiven me for beating him at chess and so he made me your guardian in retribution," Richard added, continuing the game. "But it won't work. I shall simply approve everything you do and wash my hands of all responsibility!"

"Good, then I may be as outrageous as I choose," Drusilla retorted. "I wonder if I have time to damp my muslins before I go out tonight?"

"Do so and I shall personally administer to you the sound thrashing you would well deserve," Pensley told her with a growl.

"But why? Everyone does it," Drusilla protested innocently.

"Everyone who doesn't care a fig for their reputation," Richard told her grimly.

"But I'm a widow. I may do as I please," Drusilla persisted, her eyes dancing.

Pensley drew the horses to a halt and looked down at Drusilla, his eyes meeting hers as he said, "If you so much as dare to damp your muslins, I repeat that I shall give you the thrashing you so richly deserve. Whatever the reason Hugo had for naming me your caretaker, he did so, and I intend to see that you do nothing to ruin yourself."

The stern words were belied, however, by the twitching at the corner of Pensley's lips, and after a moment he too laughed. "Poor Hugo," he said. "I've no doubt you drove him to distraction before he died."

"On the contrary," Drusilla protested, "I nursed him around the clock and hadn't time to think of getting into trouble."

"Otherwise, no doubt you would have," Richard retorted.

Drusilla laughed. "Perhaps. But I really am not the flighty creature you seem to think me. I may joke about damping my muslins, but I would not do it."

"No, you would be afraid of catching your death of pneumonia after living so long in such a warm climate," he retorted.

"Precisely," she agreed cordially.

Pensley shook his head. "Very well, I acquit you of absolute flightiness and assume that my responsibility does not extend to teaching you propriety, merely to keeping away the fortune-hunters."

"And bringing me into favor," Drusilla suggested innocently.

"You know very well you are enjoying far more success than is good for you, Mrs. Lawford," he told her severely, "and I have no intention of adding to it."

"Except by taking me out in your carriage today," Drusilla pointed out helpfully. "You must know that will do my credit no end of good."

Pensley gave a false sigh. He turned his face upward and said in mock despair, "Dear Hugo, whatever did I do to deserve this?"

They both laughed. Then feeling quite in charity

with each other, Pensley and Drusilla Lawford drove once more around the still relatively deserted park before he took her home. For it was, they both agreed, such an exceptionally fine day.

14

It was as she was out walking with Farnham that the first intimation of disaster occurred. Lady Pontworth cut Drusilla dead. "I say," Farnham thundered as that lady ignored the civil greeting Drusilla extended to her, "how dare she treat you that way?"

"Perhaps she didn't hear me?" Drusilla suggested hopefully.

"Not a bit of it," Farnham retorted impatiently. "She has the hearing of a . . . a cat or something. Overhears things no one would expect her to and to which she ought not to be listening anyway. No, she cut you just now, and dashed uncivil it was of her."

"Well, no doubt it is some sort of misunderstanding," Drusilla said equably, "for I can think of no way in which I could have offended her."

But it was not merely Lady Pontworth. Three times ladies of the *ton* refused to acknowledge Drusilla's greeting, and one went so far as to pointedly greet Farnham instead.

"Dash it all! One can't go on simply ignoring this," he said in exasperation as that lady left them.

"I-I quite agree," Drusilla answered shaken. "I think you'd best take me home now. Perhaps Mrs. Lawford will know what this is about."

"Just the ticket," Farnham said. "Seems to know about everything going on, Mrs. Lawford does. She'll know what to do. Must say, it seems deuced unlikely for anyone to take you in dislike."

"Well, perhaps we shall soon know the reason," Drusilla replied.

Neither felt much in the mood for conversation, but Farnham did his best to distract Drusilla from what had occurred. Nevertheless, after still one more member of the *ton* had refused to notice them, he too fell silent. Thus they were a gloomy pair when they reached the Lawford town house. Drusilla's first question to the footman who opened the door was "Is Mrs. Lawford at home?"

"She has just returned, I believe, ma'am," he replied impassively, "and may be found in the drawing room."

"Thank you," Drusilla said. "Please come with me, Lord Farnham. I find I am suddenly a trifle afraid."

" 'Course I'll come with you," he answered stoutly. "Shan't desert you now."

Elizabeth Lawford was indeed in the drawing room and so was her son, Julian. Their faces were quite grim as they greeted Drusilla and Farnham. Without preamble she asked, "Elizabeth, do *you* know what has occurred? I have been given the cut direct by no fewer than four members of the *ton*."

Farnham coughed. "Five," he corrected her discreetly.

Mother and son looked at each other helplessly. At last Julian said, "Rumor would have it that you are not married to my Uncle Hugo. Were not married to him. That both the story and the will were all a hum."

"What?" Drusilla felt her legs start to give way

under her, and utterly pale she sat in the nearest chair.

Elizabeth came forward and took Drusilla's hands in her own. "I'm so sorry, my dear, that you must go through this. It seems a certain lady, a Mrs. Crowley, has just returned from India. She says that her husband was stationed near your father and that she was there when your parents and my brother-in-law died. She says there was no marriage and that you and another person concocted everything between yourselves."

"But that's a lie," Drusilla protested.

"Of course it is," Elizabeth said soothingly, "but you are so pretty and have enjoyed such a success here that there are a good many jealous tongues eager to believe and spread the story."

"But how can they?" Drusilla asked. "They must know Nicholson would have checked out my story before accepting me as Hugo's wife."

Julian coughed discreetly, then said, "Well, as to that, I'm afraid it is being said that Nicholson's head was turned by your pretty face and ready tears."

"Now just a moment—" Farnham began indignantly.

Julian held up a hand. "Peace, Osbert! Your feelings do you credit, but *I* am not the one maligning my Aunt Drusilla. I am merely telling her what is being said, for I believe she ought to be forewarned."

"What I don't understand," Drusilla said, bewildered, "is why this Mrs. Crowley should gain such a ready audience. Have I truly made so many enemies here in London?" Elizabeth looked away. "Please, I should like to know," Drusilla said with dignity.

Elizabeth could not meet Drusilla's eyes as she replied, "No, it is not that. Apparently Mrs. Crowley had been telling her story for some days before anyone could credit it. But then someone started asking questions and . . . and the answers are not apparent."

"Questions?" Drusilla asked with a deadly quiet voice.

Julian answered for his mother. "I don't, for a moment, credit them," he said, "but here they are. First, if your father had died, who performed the marriage? Surely there would not have been two missionaries at one remote station. Second, why were none of these documents in Uncle Hugo's own hand? Even his signature is astonishingly shaky. Third, why did none of Uncle Hugo's servants accompany you home? It is not the thing for a lady, even a widow, to make such a journey alone. Fourth, why such odd terms to his will? They were far more favorable to you than anyone might have expected. Fifth, fifth is why should he have married you at all when he could, at most, have known you for only a few weeks? Uncle Hugo was not the sort of man to marry on an impulse. Indeed, there are many in the *ton* who have heard him swear never to marry at all. Sixth, well that shall do for now."

Drusilla looked around the room at the strained faces of her friends. Even Farnham's had lost its color. "I see," she said at last. "You have not asked for answers; nevertheless, I should like to give them to you."

Hastily Elizabeth said, "Hush! Surely you must know there is no need? *We* do not question your marriage. No, save such nonsense for the *ton*. Here you are safe and welcome, always. Why don't you go upstairs and rest a bit? This has been a shock to you, I am certain."

"But I should like to answer," Drusilla repeated quietly.

"No, I refuse to hear of it," Julian said emphatically. "You are not under suspicion here and I refuse to allow you to behave as if you were."

Drusilla looked at Farnham, who hastily said, "Yes, yes, by all means do go upstairs and rest, Mrs. Lawford. No need to explain anything to us. We believe you."

"Very well," she said, rising to her feet, "I shan't argue any further. Now, at any rate. Later, however, we must speak of this."

"Anything you wish," Elizabeth assured her. "But do go upstairs now and have your maid bathe your temples with scented water. I am persuaded it will do you a world of good."

A trifle unsteadily Drusilla left the room. When she was gone, Elizabeth turned to Farnham and said, "Thank you for your kindness toward my dear sister-in-law. This is a terrible time and one cannot help but feel for her. Those questions! One doesn't want to worry about them, but one cannot help it."

Farnham, who was not terribly bright, nevertheless understood enough to ask, "Would it not have been better, perhaps, to allow her to answer those questions, Mrs. Lawford?"

"To be sure, Osbert," Julian said, leaning against the fireplace, hands in his pockets, "*if* one could be certain her answers would be adequate. In this instance, however, I think it best she, we all, maintain a dignified silence."

Farnham colored and nodded. "Quite right. I'd for-gotten, of course, that you must know more than I about all this. Oh, dear, dear, what a position to be in! I-I think I'd best go now."

"Do we see you at Lord and Lady Denley's party tonight?" Elizabeth asked brightly.

"Are . . . are you going?" Farnham asked with some surprise.

"Of course," Julian replied with a frown. "I'll be damned if I'll allow us to hide at home as though there were some truth to these rumors."

"Of course," Farnham said.

"I repeat, do we see you there?" Elizabeth asked him mildly.

"Yes, no, that is, I am not certain," Farnham said, flustered. "I—"

"That is quite all right," Julian said with dreadful irony. "We understand perfectly. Mother, you were quite tactless to press the fellow when he has not yet made up his mind as to whether or not he believes Aunt Drusilla's story."

"That's not what I meant," Farnham protested.

Elizabeth Lawford drew herself to her full height and regarded her visitor thunderously. "That will do, Lord Farnham. I know precisely what to think. You may go, and I take leave to tell you frankly that you are not welcome here unless and until you are able to accept fully Drusilla as my brother-in-law's rightful widow."

Farnham lost no time in departing.

When he was gone, Elizabeth Lawford and her son regarded each other steadily for a moment and then raised imaginary glasses in a toast to each other.

Upstairs, Annie was bathing Drusilla's temples as Elizabeth had suggested. In that mysterious way that servants have of knowing everything, Annie had already heard of the accusations. "Imagine anyone doubting you," she said indignantly. "I should like to give this Mrs. Crowley a piece of my mind. Probably putting on airs far above her station and wanting to get a bit of notice by creating a scandal and thinking there'll be nothing you can do to touch her. A good hiding, that's what she needs. And I, for one, should like to give it to her."

In spite of herself, Drusilla laughed. "I do believe you mean it," she said.

"Of course I do," Annie said indignantly. "The idea of spreading such a tale! Anyone looking at you must know you'd never do such a thing."

With a sigh, Drusilla said, "How I wish everyone were as kind and loyal as you are, Annie. I fear, however, that the *ton* is only too ready to believe the worst of everyone."

Both women fell silent. After several minutes Annie said diffidently, "Perhaps, ma'am, we ought to go back to Mr. Lawford's country house. There wouldn't be so many people there who have heard the story."

Drusilla sat up. Meeting Annie's eyes directly, she said, "I shouldn't be too certain of that. It's my experience that tales such as this spread with an astonishing speed. No, we can't hide from it that way."

"Nor you don't want to hide from it," Annie observed shrewdly. "You're the sort would rather stay and fight, wouldn't you, ma'am? And like it!"

"Fight, yes. Like it, no," Drusilla said bluntly. "Having lived among the military, however, one quickly learns that it is fatal to turn one's back upon the enemy. I shan't let myself or Hugo be abused this way. I am his wife because he wanted it so, and so the world shall know."

"Aye, the problem is, will they believe it?" Annie asked with a shake of her head.

"That I don't know," Drusilla conceded. "But given time, they must. Surely even the *ton* must realize that if Nocholson accepts me as Hugo's widow, he must have reason. And he has not yet doubted my story." She paused, then added with another sigh, "At any rate, not since shortly after my return. *He* found my answers adequate."

"What about Lord Pensley?" Annie wondered aloud. "He could do you a world of good if he supported your claim."

"Lord Pensley. Certainly he could, if he chose to," Drusilla agreed. "The difficulty is, I don't know what he will do when he hears Mrs. Crowley's claims. He has already told me, more than once, that he did not understand why Hugo married me, that the story I told him did not make sense."

15

At that very moment Lord Pensley stood in Nicholson's office.

"You are very good to come so promptly, m'lord. Please be seated," the solicitor said politely, gesturing toward a chair. "I should not have inconvenienced you like this except that I was afraid that if I were seen arriving at your town house, it might cause more talk than is already occurring. And in a situation as delicate as this, well, I should like to avoid that at all costs."

Lord Pensley leaned back in the chair. He was as neatly, if not more neatly, attired as he would have been had he been calling on a member of the *ton*. Even Nicholson could have told at a glance that his coat had been made by Weston, his fawn-colored trousers fitted by an expert, the cravat tied in no less than half an hour of effort, and his dark locks brushed with care.

With a deprecating wave of his hand Pensley said, "You have not inconvenienced me in the slightest. I confess, however, I am a trifle confused as to the matter in hand. I should have thought all my affairs well in order."

"So they are, so they are," Nicholson agreed hastily. "This matter concerns Mrs., er, the lady who calls herself Mrs. Lawford."

Astonishment showed on Pensley's face. "The lady who calls herself Mrs. Lawford?" he repeated incredulously. "What the devil do you mean by that?"

Nicholson cleared his throat. "I should not like to be responsible for helping to perpetuate possibly unfounded rumors, m'lord, however, a certain Mrs. Crowley has raised questions as to the authenticity of the marriage of Miss Drusilla Crandall to Mr. Hugo Lawford and of the will supposedly written after this event." Nicholson paused and then said delicately, "You have, I presume, heard these rumors? If not, I am sorry to shock you as I am persuaded this must do."

Again Pensley waved a hand, this time impatiently. "Yes, yes, I had heard such rumors, but I assumed them to be mere nonsense. Good God, man, you've met Drusilla Lawford. Surely you cannot imagine her to be guilty of such a fraud?"

Nicholson hesitated. "Well, as to that, m'lord, I should not care to say. In any event, my opinion does not matter. You must see that it is my duty to investigate such a charge, whatever my personal feelings. I should be irresponsible if I did not consider the possibility that they were true."

"I do see," Richard said, regarding Nicholson from beneath a furrowed brow. "And as fellow trustee of Hugo's estate, the responsibility is mine as well."

"Precisely," Nicholson said, pleased to be so easily understood. "Moreover, m'lord, you are in a far better position than I to speak to—"

"Mrs. Lawford," Richard said. "We owe her that courtesy unless events prove us mistaken."

"Yes, indeed," Nicholson agreed, "Mrs. Lawford. You are in a far better position to speak to her than I am. Meanwhile I have already begun certain investigations of my own. They will take time, but perhaps we will have an answer sooner than we expect."

"Discreet investigations, I hope," Pensley said.

Indignation warred with respect upon Nicholson's face. Outrage won. "My dear Lord Pensley, I have been a solicitor for over twenty-five years. I trust I know what circumspection is due my clients. That is precisely the reason I have asked you to speak to Mrs. Lawford. If you are seen entering or leaving my office, it may be believed you have come to consult me about your own affairs. But as matters stand, if Mrs. Lawford is seen speaking to me at all, it will seem as though the rumors have been confirmed."

"My apologies," Richard said meekly.

"Thank you," Nicholson replied. "Now, here is a list of the questions that are being asked concerning Mrs. Lawford's marriage." He handed a sheet of papers covered in neat handwriting to Lord Pensley, who looked them over carefully.

"You are remarkably well-informed," Richard said at last, his face impassive. "May I ask where you heard these questions?"

Stiffly Nicholson replied, "I did not hear them, m'lord. Those questions on that paper were delivered to these offices yesterday. I spent all night considering what ought to be done about them. They are one more reason this situation cannot be ignored, even should we wish to do so. Someone knows these questions have been given to me, and for Mrs. Lawford's sake as well as my late client Mr. Hugo Lawford, the matter must be resolved."

"You are quite right," Richard agreed. "I should give a great deal to know who delivered them—or rather, who caused them to be delivered."

The two men looked at each other and Nicholson

coughed discreetly. "It is not my place to conjecture," he said. "However, it occurs to me there are two individuals who might be very interested in such a charge."

"My thoughts precisely," Richard said with a smile that held no amusement. "I presume you have had in mind that I should also find it easier to observe these two individuals than for you to do so?"

"You are remarkably perceptive, my lord," Nicholson answered, inclining his head slightly.

"All right," Pensley said, rising to his feet, "I shall do as you ask and send you round a note if I discover anything."

Nicholson had also risen. "Thank you, my lord. And I shall notify you at once should my investigations provide an answer."

In perfect accord, they bid each other good day and Pensley set out for the Lawford town house. The footman there tried to inform him that Mrs. Drusilla Lawford was not at home, but Pensley refused to allow it. Pushing his way past the fellow, he called over his shoulder, "Then I shall just wait for her in the library."

Helpless, the poor footman showed Lord Pensley into that small room and then went in search of his mistress. Left alone, Pensley ignored the minor collection of books and stared grimly out the window. He did not have long to wait. Scarcely five minutes after he had been shown into the library, the door of the room opened and he turned to see Elizabeth Lawford standing there with a look of thunderous anger upon her face.

"May I ask why you have had the effrontery to force your way into my home?" she demanded icily.

"I wish to speak with your sister-in-law," he answered coldly.

"She is indisposed," Elizabeth replied.

"I wish to speak with her," Pensley repeated implacably. "If she will not come down, then I shall go up to her, but I will speak with her."

"Upon what matter?" Elizabeth demanded, changing tactics.

Richard faced her directly as he said, "Upon the charge that she is not, in fact, Mrs. Lawford but still Miss Drusilla Crandall."

"My lord," Elizabeth Lawford gasped, "I protest. I will not have you speak to my dear sister-in-law that way."

"No?" Pensley asked silkily. "I warn you—officially as a trustee of your late brother-in-law's estate—that if she will not speak to me about this matter, then she will soon be speaking with representatives of the law."

Elizabeth Lawford hesitated. After a moment she said, chastened, "I shall go and get Drusilla."

Pensley bowed. As she turned to go, he stopped her. With the same silky voice he said, "I wish to speak with your supposed sister-in-law alone, Mrs. Lawford. And, Mrs. Lawford . . ."

"Yes?"

"If I discover that so much as a whisper has leaked out about my visit here today I shall hold you directly accountable and I assure you that you will greatly regret it."

"You may trust my discretion," she said stiffly.

Again Pensley bowed, and this time he let her go. He did not see but would not have been surprised at the smile upon her face as she closed the door behind her.

A few minutes later the door opened again and this time Drusilla entered the library. Her eyes were more than a little strained and she twisted a handkerchief in her hands as she said, "You wished to see me, Lord Pensley?"

"Please be seated," he said in a far kinder tone than he had used with her sister-in-law.

Drusilla did so, forcing herself to meet his eyes as she asked, "You have come, I presume, about Mrs. Crowley's accusations?"

"Yes, I have," Richard replied, his face now impassive. He paused and waited for a moment before he said sharply, "Who performed the marriage? At the time that it took place your father had been assigned to a remote station. The sort of station where there would have been no more than one pastor or missionary assigned to it. And you have told me yourself that your father died *before* the marriage took place."

Drusilla looked at him coolly. "You think you have me there, don't you?" She leaned forward. "Well, you are wrong! You have forgotten what I have told you more than once. My father went to India before clerics were allowed to work openly there. He went as an employee of the East India Company in an entirely secular post. Therefore he was *not* the churchman for our station, only one more unofficial missionary, one that the Company could claim no knowledge of. The marriage was performed by Reverend Amesley, as the papers I gave Mr. Nicholson expressly state."

Pensley inclined his head. "Very well, that can be verified. Perhaps. But why did Hugo's servants refuse to come with you when you returned to England? Surely if you were actually Hugo's wife they would have felt a responsibility to you as well? And where are they now? Why have they not returned, unless it is out of a dislike of seeing you installed at Lawford Manor or because you have bribed them not to return and expose you?"

Drusilla closed her eyes, then opened them. Mirthlessly she laughed. "My dear Lord Pensley, have you forgotten, or did you never know, that Hugo's personal servants were Indian? After his death they would have returned to England with me, feeling, as you have said, that it was their duty to do so, but *I* felt I could not let them. Would you? I asked them, you see, which climate they preferred. Which homeland. I asked whether any of them had a family in India they wished to return to. Are you surprised that all of them wished to stay there? It was my insistence that I could travel alone, my assurance that they need not feel themselves bound to me, which allowed them to remain. My God, it never occurred to me that one day I should be called to account for placing their wishes above useless propriety. I asked of them only that they accompany me to Bombay and wait there with me until I could board a ship to England before they dispersed to their homes. They were grateful for that, you know."

His face impassive, Pensley said, "Can you explain the will as well? The terms that are, to society, so odd? The bulk of Hugo's wealth left to a wife he had scarcely had time to come to know? Particularly a will that is, none of it, written in Hugo's own hand? And with a signature so shaky I should scarcely like to swear to its authenticity?"

"I have told you before I cannot explain the will," she cried out. "And if I wrote the will, wishing to steal the fortune from Julian, why should I have put in that absurd provision that gave *you* approval over whom I may and may not wed?"

"That was clever, I will allow," he replied maddeningly.

"You are a fool," Drusilla flung at him, striking the arm of her chair with her fist. "You know I would not have done such a thing."

"Not unless you supposed me to have more hair than wit, someone whom you could deceive into approving whomever you wished to marry," Richard agreed.

Seething, Drusilla replied, "I cannot change your mind, for obviously you have made certain of your opinion. Very well, but I still tell you I did not write the will; it was Hugo's words, written down by Reverend Amesley. The same Amesley who married us. Written down for Hugo because he was too ill to take up a pen and write the thing himself. I have told you he was dying of cholera and that is why his signature was so shaky." She paused, glaring at Pensley. Then, when he did not speak, she demanded goadingly, "Aren't you going to ask why he married me? That is something else everyone seems to find astonishing. As you told me the first day we met, Hugo was wont to tell everyone he never intended to marry."

Dryly he replied, "I have already heard your version of that story, remember?"

"Ah, yes, when we went out riding in your carriage," Drusilla said airily. "How clever of me to answer that question in advance." He did not answer and once more she prodded him. "Go on. I feel sure you must have more questions. Pray, don't spare them out of consideration for my feelings."

"I shan't," he said briefly. "And you are correct, I

do have more. With whom did you travel on the ship? Can you prove that you were ever in India at all?" Drusilla gasped but Pensley went on inexorably, "Can you even prove that you are, or were, Drusilla Crandall? Can you prove that you did not murder Hugo by poison? Can you prove that Amesley was not in your employ when he wrote out the marriage lines for you? Can you even prove that he is a lawful clergyman empowered to preside over a marriage? Can you prove anything?"

Stunned, she could only stare at him, her face even paler than before, if such a thing were possible. "Are you mad?" she asked at last.

"I am merely repeating the questions that are being whispered about and that have been given to Nicholson by some unknown citizen," Pensley said impassively. After a moment he took pity upon her and spoke more gently, "Come, I do not expect you to be able to answer me now. These are matters Nicholson can and must try to investigate. I am more concerned with discovering who can hate you so thoroughly that they would do such a thing."

"I don't know," Drusilla replied, her voice scarcely above a whisper. "I don't even know who Mrs. Crowley is."

"I shall find that out," Richard retorted, "but you probably don't know her. I presume she was bribed by someone to make these accusations."

"But who?" Drusilla demanded.

"That, I don't know," Pensley repeated grimly, "but as I said, I intend to find out."

Drusilla breathed a sigh of relief and stood up. "So you are my friend, after all. I had begun to wonder, you know, just now."

Pensley looked down at her, a twisted smile upon

his lips. "It would have done you no good for me to coddle you," he said. "If I am to help you, I need as many answers as you can give me, for I am certain to be asked my opinions as well."

"I wish Elizabeth and Julian understood that," Drusilla told him with a sigh. "They have been so kind and so determined to support me, but they do not understand that something must be said. The only thing upon which we are in agreement is that I must not flee London or avoid the *ton* as though I were indeed guilty."

Pensley nodded. "In that they are correct." He paused, "I do stand as your friend and will do what I can to help you. Shall you be at Lord and Lady Denley's ball tonight?" Drusilla nodded and he said in a gentle voice, "I'll see you there, then. But now I must be off."

"Good-bye," she said, "and thank you."

In answer Richard kissed Drusilla lightly and then, before she could recover from her astonishment, was gone.

16

It quickly became borne in upon Drusilla that the disaster would *not* simply disappear, edged out by some newer, more scandalous story among the *ton*. Too many people, it seemed, gave credence to Mrs. Crowley's charges. At Lord and Lady Denley's ball Drusilla's loss of acceptance all but went unnoticed in the greater excitement over the announced betrothal between some American chit and Sir Stacey Warfield. Except that Drusilla noticed her beaux, such as Farnham and Thornley and Braden and Dunsworth, had all deserted her. Not that she had ever taken Dunsworth seriously, for at times he seemed almost a misogynist. And the the others were more heedless boys, in Drusilla's eyes, than anything else. Still, Drusilla was too intelligent not to realize that these desertions were a harbinger of what was to come. And she was correct.

Several mornings later, deeply distressed, Elizabeth Lawford contemplated the pile of invitations that had arrived. Though she did not look forward to further humiliation, Drusilla forced herself to ask brightly, "Well, where do we go tonight?"

Elizabeth hesitated. At last she said, "We-we don't. I am much fatigued, my dear, and thought we might spend a quiet evening at home."

"Gammon!" her son said. "You've never spent a quiet evening at home by choice in your life, Mother."

Hastily Elizabeth threw her son a warning frown and said, "Yes, but I have never had so bad a headache before, either."

They were seated at the breakfast table and now Julian rose, holding out his hand imperatively. "Let me see those invitations, Mother," he said quietly.

She did as he asked, and Drusilla watched silently. Somehow it came as no surprise to her when he at last laid down the pile of invitations and said angrily, "They've no right to be so rude. I shan't allow it. Aunt Drusilla will come with us or we go nowhere."

"My sentiments precisely," Elizabeth said approvingly.

Her throat tight, Drusilla said, "I collect my presence is unwelcome at London parties just now."

Reluctantly Elizabeth nodded. Julian, however, snapped his fingers and said, "That is how little I value the opinion of the *ton*, at least in so far as it concerns you, Aunt Drusilla. *I* do not doubt that Uncle Hugo married you for good and sufficient reasons."

"Perhaps I had best go back to the country," Drusilla began.

But Elizabeth and Julian would have none of it. "You cannot simply admit defeat," she protested. "If we put our heads together, surely we shall contrive something. Perhaps if we wait long enough, everyone will simply forget these absurd charges."

Drusilla leaned back in her chair and said, "I think not. Particularly as it has somehow become known that even Hugo's solicitor has begun an investigation of my credentials."

"Yes, but Lord Pensley supports you," Elizabeth pointed out.

Drusilla nodded. "So he does, and I have begun to hear it said that he is simply a fool. His credit has not helped me, but mine has hurt him."

"Fustian," Julian said, pacing impatiently. "You may believe me when I say that Pensley's credit is well able to sustain such absurd assaults upon it." Abruptly he turned and placed his hands on the table across from Drusilla. "You must not run from the *ton*," he said. "Come, let us snap our fingers at them together. We shall go to Vauxhall Gardens tonight and be seen laughing as though we have not a care in the world."

Drusilla started to refuse, but when she saw Julian and Elizabeth looking at her so hopefully, she could not. "Very well," she said with a sigh, "we shall go."

At that same moment, ironically, Lord Pensley was making similar plans. He had promised Arabella Fletcher, some time past, that he would take her to Vauxhall Gardens, and at last the weather seemed warm enough and calm enough to do so. Like Julian, Richard sent someone round to make all the arrangements. And yet Pensley felt a grim foreboding about the evening ahead. He could not shake the fear that Arabella expected him to propose to her that night. When he confided this fear to Cordelia, her solution was simple. "I shall go with you," she said. "Even Arabella cannot expect you to speak when I am there."

"There are too many darkened pathways," Pensley observed impatiently. "She will find a way for us to be alone."

"So there are," came the maddeningly calm reply, "but you need not fall in with her plans."

Lord Pensley was still not satisfied, however. "I ought never to have invited her," he said. "I ought to have seen this coming."

"So you ought," his sister agreed. "Everyone else did."

Startled, Pensley looked at his sister. "You are roasting me, Cordelia, aren't you?"

"Not a bit of it," she replied placidly. "Men may be blind, but we women are not and more than I have guessed Arabella Fletcher meant to marry you." Patience gave way to exasperation as Cordelia demanded, "Well, what *did* you think was the reason for Arabella's constant presence in your country house and her constant contrivance to be in your company here?"

Pensley looked at his sister. Levelly he said, "Arabella lost her husband as I lost Sarah. I had no notion matters went beyond that."

"Men!" Cordelia snorted. "Well, you may depend upon it that Arabella assumes that you knew how she felt, and that, had the notion been distasteful to you, then you would have hinted her away a long time ago."

For several moments Richard was silent. At last he said, "It's true that there was a time when I would have welcomed her as my wife, but now I cannot. I shall have to speak with her tonight and tell her how I feel. So you need not come along, after all, Cordelia."

"To the contrary," his sister retorted, "you shall need me more than ever. Unless you enjoy the experience of having a lady become a watering pot and use your best coat as a place against which to cry."

"Good God, no," Richard exclaimed.

"Then it's all settled," Cordelia said with more than a little satisfaction. "I shall accompany you tonight, and you may rest assured that if your words do not have the desired effect, mine will."

"What words?" her brother asked suspiciously.

But Cordelia refused to answer, turning the topic with a coolness that infuriated him. "How is Drusilla getting on?" she asked.

"Tolerably well," Richard said stiffly.

"Indeed?" Cordelia raised an eyebrow in disbelief. "I find that difficult to credit. The tattleboxes have found more than their share to wag their tongues about on this story. I have heard it said with great authority—always, of course, by the most foolish of women—that Mrs. Lawford is known incontrovertibly to have murdered her husband, Hugo Lawford, and also that the evidence is absolute that she never married him at all." At this point Cordelia dropped her mask of foolishness and said seriously, "Is the case as hard as it seems, Richard?"

"Worse," he said grimly. "Nicholson cannot quite decide what to believe, and there is pressure for him to turn everything over to young Julian as the previous will required."

"But surely he does not believe this ... this calumny?" Cordelia demanded. "Surely he is investigating to clear Mrs. Lawford's name?"

Pensley nodded. "Yes, he is. But investigations take a great deal of time. Especially when they involve a marriage which may or may not have taken place so very far away as a remote company station in India. I am afraid the investigation could take a year. Nicholson is mysteriously sure it will not."

"Poor Drusilla," Cordelia murmured. "How fortunate, however, that she has you in her corner."

Richard did not answer directly. Instead, he said, "Do you know, Wainscott told me yesterday that he thought I must be in my dotage to accept the 'fairy tale,' as he called it, that Drusilla is telling."

"What did you say?" Cordelia asked, genuinely curious.

"I observed that I had not heard Hugo's sister-in-law, Elizabeth Lawford, or his nephew, Julian, question her claim to be Hugo's widow," Richard replied.

"And what did Wainscott say to that?" Cordelia persisted.

Richard shrugged angrily. "He said that since 'that woman' was their houseguest, they could scarcely turn her out or speak against her and that everyone among the *ton* felt for them."

"What nonsense," Cordelia exclaimed indignantly.

"Just so," Pensley agreed. "Unfortunately it is very clever nonsense."

"What do you mean?" Cordelia asked cautiously.

"Oh, come, Cordelia," her brother retorted impatiently, "you have never been lacking in wits! Who stands most to gain should Drusilla's marriage to Hugo be declared a fraud?"

"Julian and Elizabeth Lawford," Cordelia conceded reluctantly.

"Agreed," Richard said curtly. "You will allow, will you not, that they are clever enough to have found and bribed someone like Mrs. Crowley to spread such a tale?"

"But they have been so kind to her," Cordelia started to protest. She broke off, however, and said, "Yes, I see. But what can you do about it?"

Pensley regarded his sister steadily. "Tomorrow I call upon Mrs. Crowley and try to discover if she can either be bribed or threatened into telling who paid her to do this, and whether she can be persuaded to publicly renounce her prior words."

Cordelia nodded. After a moment she said, "Freddie must be quite angry at all this trouble, or have you kept the news from him?"

"Kept the news from him?" Pensley asked in mock astonishment. "My dear sister, that would be impossible. Even had I not told him, he must have heard it from the servants or from one of his friends. No, he came to me several days ago and asked if it was true that some people were saying Drusilla had never married Hugo. When I confessed that it was, I swear the boy was prepared to challenge the entire *ton* to a duel. And when I forbade *that* on the grounds of his tender age, he was inclined to feel that I ought to do so for him."

"For Drusilla, you mean," Cordelia pointed out with a laugh. "Well? What did you tell Freddie?"

"That I would not do it, of course," Richard replied coolly. "He was inclined to think me a very poor-spirited fellow until I explained that to do so would in no way aid Mrs. Lawford's reputation and might, indeed, damage it further."

"Did he accept that?" Cordelia asked, a twinkle in her eye.

"He had to," Pensley retorted. "But I notice that he has more than once come home since then showing signs of having been in a brawl with the other boys hereabouts."

Cordelia regarded her brother, a speculative look upon her face. "I wonder if Drusilla appreciates such champions to her cause."

"I think perhaps she does," he replied, a rare smile upon his face.

Arabella Fletcher was inclined to agree. Indeed, had anyone asked her, she might have said that Mrs. Lawford was far too appreciative of the brief courtesy that Lord Pensley had extended toward her and that was why she was inclined to . . . to positively throw herself at him so offensively. And her attentiveness to Pensley's son was merely one way of gaining his lordship's favor. Of course, Arabella only said this in the strictest of confidence to one or two of her dearest friends and only after being asked her opinion of Mrs. Lawford's claim to widowhood and Lord Pensley's support of that claim. Nevertheless, it somehow came about that most of the *ton* heard how Arabella Fletcher felt.

Unfortunately for Arabella, most people were correctly inclined to attribute her words to jealousy, for while it might explain Drusilla Lawford's attentiveness to Pensley, it did not explain his to her. Nor were her dear friends loath to tell Arabella how others felt. Thus Arabella was not in the happiest of moods as she prepared for the evening at the Vauxhall Gardens.

17

Arabella Fletcher was not a stupid woman. She understood very well that she was in danger of losing Lord Pensley. The unkind would say she never had possessed him, but Arabella knew that there had been a time when Pensley would have asked for her hand in marriage had she pushed him. At that point, however, she had still been too fond of her newfound freedom to want marriage, and now it looked as if it might be too late.

A lesser woman would have conceded defeat and looked elsewhere for a spouse, particularly as a certain retired colonel had recently indicated an interest in her. But Arabella was not a lesser woman; she was a supremely confident one. Yes, Pensley's thoughts had begun to wander elsewhere, but Arabella had been Lady Pensley's best friend and knew a great many details no one else understood.

She knew, for example, that it was at Vauxhall Gardens that Lord Pensley had first proposed marriage to Sarah, even though it was two weeks later, at a ball, that she had given her consent. She knew his favorite foods, wines, and her dresses had been chosen with an eye to his favorite colors. And if that were not enough, Arabella constantly, if quietly, reminded Lord Pensley that, like his dear Sarah, she was a devoted mother. Had it been possible, she would have brought her son, Peter, to Vauxhall Gardens the evening she hoped to prompt Pensley to propose. Ah, well, if Peter were not there, then neither would Freddie be, and he was no help to her campaign.

It was scarcely an accident, therefore, that Arabella chose a dress of a striking shade of green cambric with only a bit of lace about the bosom, matching gloves and shoes, as well as a new confection of straw and lace and silk flowers to wear upon her head. The price of this toilette was quite dear, but Arabella viewed that in the nature of an investment.

The merest hint of "spanish wool" colored her cheeks, alkanna root her lips, and elderberry extract her eyebrows. So delicately were these applied that Arabella was safe in presuming that neither Lord Pensley nor any other gentleman would guess she had resorted to such artifice. Then, although Pensley had already arrived, Arabella sat down to wait a full ten minutes before she descended the stairs to greet him. Tonight she would *not* appear eager.

Indeed, so well had Arabella schooled herself for tonight's campaign that nothing about her showed that she considered Lady Ratherby's presence to be a severe setback. Instead, she was all graciousness, quietly complimenting Cordelia's dress and then making a show of leaving precise instructions to the staff concerning her son, Peter.

"Quite as though they have had no experience of such things at all, when everyone knows she leaves him alone six nights out of seven," Cordelia whispered to her brother indignantly.

But Lord Pensley was all patience, not betraying

by the least word or expression that he found Arabella's behavior annoying. He did, it is true, decline to enter the gardens by hiring a scull to carry them across the river, but he did so with a careless grace and Arabella took the reverse in good part. And the dinner he had ordered included, apart from the famous shaved ham and rum punch, neatly cooked pullets and tarts and any number of other dishes. Even the sight of Drusilla Lawford, in a box across the way from their own could not distress Arabella, particularly given the attentiveness of Julian Lawford. In fact, Arabella was quite convinced of the success of her scheme when Lord Pensley at last suggested he and Arabella stroll along one of the lantern-lit paths that were such a popular feature of the gardens.

Her first hint of disaster was when he halted, near one of the many fountains, and said, "I'm afraid I have deceived you, Mrs. Fletcher."

"Mrs. Fletcher?" Arabella gasped in spite of herself. "Why do you call me that?"

Pensley bit his lower lip a moment before he went on, "I think it best."

By now Arabella had rallied and she was able to ask with admirable bravado, "I see. And how have you deceived me, Richard?"

He smiled at her with the same beguiling warmth that had made her set her cap at him in the first place, then he said, "By not telling you, some time ago, that while I like you and admire you very much, I will never marry you."

Arabella tossed her head with a laugh that was weak even to her own ears. "Indeed?" she said, determined at least to salvage her pride. "And what need was there for you to say so? Surely you do not think I was so foolish as to assume otherwise? Perhaps it is you who have misread my kindness to Sarah's widower as something more. Or my kindness to her son. We have been friends a long time, Lord Pensley, I did not look for more."

"Well, that is what I thought," Richard said candidly. "But Cordelia would have it that you had set your cap for me. And as I am not given to the greatest perceptiveness, I fear, I thought perhaps she might be right." He paused, but this time she did not answer and Richard took one of her hands in his own. "I am sorry if I have distressed you. I would not have done that for the world," he said quietly. "I admire you, and I am and shall always be grateful for your kindness to me after Sarah died. And to Freddie. If I have been so puffed up in my own conceit that I mistook your feelings for me, then pray forgive me for that as well."

Arabella nodded and gently withdrew her hand from his. Then, with eyes fixed upon the ground she asked, with a lightness that cost all her self-control, "Tell me, Lord Pensley, since that is how you prefer I should address you, why you cannot marry me. Not that I ever expected you would, but since you now seem so concerned to tell me you cannot, I confess to a desire to know why."

For a long moment he hesitated and finally Arabella raised her eyes to meet Richard's. "Well?" she said coolly. "I think I've a right to know."

Pensley colored. He had meant it when he said he never wished to hurt Arabella Fletcher. With a hint of desperation he said, "Because I-I am going to marry Drusilla Lawford."

In the stunned silence that followed, Richard discovered, to his own astonishment, that he meant what he had just said. Indeed, so startled was he that Arabella was the first to recover. "Forgive me," she said icily, "I must have overlooked the notice in the *Gazette*."

"There was no notice. In the *Gazette* or elsewhere," Richard answered evenly. "Our . . . our understanding is . . . is a secret one."

"How wise," Arabella could not resist observing. "That way, should evidence prove Mrs. Lawford to be a fraud, you may quietly withdraw your proposal. Very clever. And very clever of Mrs. Lawford. The *ton* would scarcely enjoy knowing that such a heartless charlatan had also succeeded in snaring the marriage mart's greatest prize."

Abruptly Pensley straightened and said, "But, my dear Mrs. Fletcher, you are much mistaken in naming me the greatest such prize. There are at least five gentlemen whose names immediately come to mind who must inevitably be considered far more eligible than myself."

Arabella shrugged. "Perhaps you are right," she said a trifle pettishly. "Nevertheless, Mrs. Lawford obviously is shrewd enough not to wish to arouse jealousy such as the announcement of your engagement with her would produce. You must know you have been considered a hopeless case."

"You are unfair to Mrs. Lawford," Richard retorted hotly.

"Indeed?" Arabella told him skeptically. "Then it is your caution that has prompted such secrecy. How wise of you."

"Well, there you are out," Richard told her rashly. "I should wish to marry Drusilla Lawford whatever the outcome of this absurd scandal."

Once more Pensley was startled to realize he

meant what he had just said. For a long moment
Arabella regarded him silently, reading the
resolution in his face. At last she said quietly, "Then
I think you are a bit mad, my friend. No, don't
trouble to accompany me back to the box. I shall find
my way well enough on my own. When you return,
after you have regained your composure, I trust, you
shall find me engaged in happy conversation with
your dear sister, Lady Ratherby, and no one but ourselves shall be any wiser as to our discussion here."

Pensley attempted one last apology. "Arabella, I
am sorry if—"

She cut him short ruthlessly. "No, Lord Pensley.
Nothing more. I think it best we both forget whatever emotions we may have felt toward each other
before today. I count myself fortunate to have
escaped marriage to someone who has so evidently
lost his wits, as well as his sense of propriety. You
may dress it up as you will, but either you are
engaged to Mrs. Lawford or you are not. Secret
engagements are *not* good *ton*, however common
they may be in the circles Mrs. Lawford is
accustomed to moving in."

And with that she was gone, leaving Pensley
behind to regain, as she had said, his composure. As
he stood in the semidarkness, half-lost in thought, he
suddenly became aware that a figure was hurtling
toward him, a woman evidently in distress. With
little effort Richard stepped into the path and neatly
caught her and to his astonishment realized he was
holding Drusilla Lawford.

Mrs. Lawford's recognition of him did not come so
quickly and she beat upon his chest as she cried out,
"Let me go, sir. Whatever you may think, I am not
looking for company. Please let me go."

Only when she had ceased to struggle so vigorously, exhausted by her futile efforts, did Pensley loosen his grip on Drusilla. "I did not think you were," he said evenly. "I only saw someone in distress and meant, however misguidedly, to help."

"Lord Pensley!" Drusilla said with a sharp intake of breath. "Dear God, I never meant to encounter you here."

"And why should you not?" he asked reasonably as he handed her his handkerchief when she could not find her own.

But Drusilla would not answer. When she had dried her face, he said lightly, "I repeat, why should you not encounter me? Or let me help you in your distress?"

For several long moments Drusilla looked at him, helpless to explain. How could she tell him what had occurred or the sense of humiliation she felt? What if he also turned his back upon her? Evidently Pensley guessed something of her trouble, for when it became clear she would not speak he said, "You had best tell me, you know, for I shall hear it soon enough if you don't. Unless, of course, it was a private matter such as Julian Lawford forcing unwelcome attentions upon you."

"No," Drusilla replied hastily, "it was nothing like that."

"Then, what?" Pensley demanded quietly.

As he looked at her with dark, grave eyes, Drusilla suddenly found that she did not want to carry the burden on her own shoulders anymore. In a torrent the words tumbled out of her. "Mrs. Crowley. She's here. I saw her. More to the point, she saw me. And confronted me. Came up to our box and told me, in a voice the whole world must have heard, that I was a fraud and that she could prove it. I must have fainted, for when I came 'round everyone was bending over me and Mrs. Crowley was nowhere to be seen. Julian was so kind. He . . . he suggested we walk down one of the paths until . . . until I regained my composure. As though it were as easy as that. But how could I refuse? All I could think of was to escape all those prying eyes. And we did. Julian took me to one of the summer houses and we sat down and he was so understanding. And then . . . and then . . ."

Here her courage failed her and Pensley found himself sternly prodding her, "And then what, Mrs. Lawford?"

Reluctantly Drusilla raised her eyes to meet his again. "And then Julian asked me if perhaps it wouldn't be best if I left London and relinquished all claim to Hugo's name and property, since it seemed that otherwise I must soon be publicly unmasked." Drusilla paused, then laughed harshly. "He had tried, he said, to believe in me, but now it seemed likely no one would much longer. Surely, he said, a public unmasking would be more painful for me than to quietly slip away. And how can I blame Julian? He and his mother have supported me when almost no one else would. I know he has tried to help me and been the butt of jokes because of it. How can I blame him when all appearances seem so much against me?"

Richard pressed his lips together to prevent the sharp answer that might otherwise have tumbled out. To Drusilla, however, it only seemed a sign that he too was preparing to abandon her. To forestall him she said, lifting a hand, "No, you needn't say anything, Lord Pensley. I shall not be so cruel as to force you to protestations you cannot in honesty make. Indeed, I had not meant to unburden myself upon you like this. My apologies. I shall now slip away and you may pretend I have said nothing."

Drusilla turned swiftly, but Richard was faster and she found her right hand held in his iron grip as he said, looking down at her, "On the contrary, Mrs. Lawford, you shall stay right here until I let you go. A bigger piece of nonsense I have never heard in my life! You apologize for hoping for the decency you ought, by rights, to be accorded by every mutton-headed member of the *ton*."

"Please, just let me go," Drusilla pleaded.

"Not until I am done," he told her ruthlessly. "Not until I have hammered into your featherwitted head that so far from believing in Julian Lawford's kindness toward you, I believe him to be responsible for all of Mrs. Crowley's accusations against you."

"You are mad," Drusilla whispered.

"Am I?" he retorted. "Who has a better motive? Who else stands to gain so much by seeing Hugo's will overturned? Who else is so well-placed to learn enough of your life in India to make such charges seem possible?"

Drusilla's resistance crumbled under Pensley's inexorable logic. Tears once more streamed down her cheeks as she said, "Even if what you say is true, why don't you just let me go? What you say only confirms my opinion that I must leave London as soon as I may."

To her astonishment, Richard let go of Drusilla's wrist and said, "You are quite right. In fact, I should advise you to leave that house as soon after dawn tomorrow as possible."

Rubbing her sore wrist, Drusilla looked at Pensley in utter confusion. He read all the doubt and

renewed fear there, and abruptly he drew her into
his arms. One hand gently pressed her head against
his shoulder as he told her, "No, my love, you
mistake me. I am not telling you to give up in defeat,
or that I lied when I said I believed you. I am telling
you to leave London and go back to Lawford Manor
and stay there because I believe I shall soon have the
means to clear you entirely of Mrs. Crowley's
charges. And I want you nowhere near the Lawfords
when I do so, for who knows but that in their greed
and madness they might not try to poison you,
hoping to gain Hugo's property that way."

At this Drusilla lifted her head and said sharply,
"Now you really are speaking nonsense. The
Lawfords have done nothing to threaten my safety."

"Thus far they have had no need," he reminded her
evenly. "They have chosen the safer way first. And
perhaps I am mistaken and they would not try such a
thing in any event. But I have no intention of risking
your life, my beloved, on such a gamble."

Gently Drusilla disentangled herself from
Pensley's arms. Looking at him a trifle accusingly,
she said, "What did you call me, m'lord?"

"My beloved," he answered promptly.

"You are making game of me," she said uncer-
tainly.

"Not a bit of it," Richard said, taking a step toward
her.

Hastily Drusilla backed away, putting out a hand
to hold him off. "Yes, you are. You've never given me
reason to think otherwise."

"I kissed you the other day," he answered
promptly.

"Yes, but I thought that was . . . was a moment's
aberration. Something to be forgotten."

"I have not forgotten," Richard said simply. "And I should like to do it again."

"But most of London thinks you are about to marry Arabella Fletcher," Drusilla protested weakly.

"Then most of London is wrong," Richard said coolly, continuing to advance upon her. "In fact, this very evening I have told Mrs. Fletcher that I am going to marry you."

"But you have said over and over you don't believe me when I say Hugo married me out of pity," Drusilla said. "You've stood by me, these last few days, but do you believe any of my story?"

"Most of it," he replied, moving closer still. "But Hugo didn't marry you out of pity; he married you out of admiration. I told you that before. As I intend to do."

Too stunned by this pronouncement to flee any farther, Drusilla found herself once more enveloped in Pensley's comforting arms and his mouth pressed gently upon hers. And in the moments that followed, she found she wanted things that way and it was Pensley who broke the kiss. Looking down at her with a smile she had never seen before, Richard said, "It's quite true I've not told you before how I felt, but that was because I thought you were in love with Julian Lawford."

"Julian?" Drusilla repeated in disbelief. "But I told you I wasn't. That boy? How could you think it?"

"Because I'm a fool," Pensley retorted lightly, kissing her again.

How long this might have gone on, neither Drusilla nor Richard had a chance to find out because some other couple came down the path just then. Reluctantly Pensley released her and said, waiting until the couple had passed, "You'd best go back to the Lawfords now. Tell them that you are tired and wish to go home and pack and that you plan to leave in the morning, you are not sure just where you will go. Tell them, if you wish, that you are even contemplating doing as Julian says: renouncing your claim to be Hugo's widow. But whatever you tell them, be sure you are gone as early as you can, stopping for breakfast on the road rather than eating anything more in their house. Will you do that for me?" She nodded and he went on, "Good. Then go at once to Lawford Manor and wait there until I come to tell you all is well again in London."

"All right. I shall," Drusilla said with a simplicity that delighted his lordship. "Good night."

And then she was gone and Pensley slowly made his way back to his own box.

18

Lord Pensley rose at an hour that would have appalled his friends had they known of it. Even the fact of his having returned from Vauxhall surprisingly early the night before could not have excused such eccentricity. Nor would anything short of a meeting to settle an affair of honor have sufficed to excuse the haste with which Lord Pensley dressed and consumed his breakfast.

Which was, in a way, the truth, Pensley reflected as he entered the hack he had had his servants summon, in the interest of discretion, shortly past nine in the morning. For it was a matter of honor he intended to settle with Mrs. Crowley. Though it was scarcely the usual meeting of pistols at dawn, Pensley hoped that his early descent upon the lady would so discompose her that she would be readier to admit the deception she had engaged upon.

As the driver threaded his way through the uncrowded streets of early-morning London, Pensley found himself wondering what he would do if he could not succeed in shaking Mrs. Crowley's story. By the time he had arrived at the Winslow Hotel, he had still reached no firm conclusion beyond the determination to clear Drusilla Lawford's name.

The clerk at the desk was inclined to hesitate to

disturb Mrs. Crowley quite so early, and had it been anyone less, er, lordly, as he later told the under-clerk, he would most certainly have refused to do so. As it was, however, a young boy was dispatched upstairs with the intriguing note Pensley had had the foresight to write out before leaving home. Within minutes the reply was brought that Mrs. Crowley would be pleased to receive his lordship in half an hour. Pensley thanked the boy, tipped him gener-ously, then sat again in a corner to wait.

Promptly at the time appointed, Pensley rapped on the door of Mrs. Crowley's suite. A sallow-faced companion opened the door. "Yes?" she said doubt-fully.

"I am Lord Pensley," he said with a cool bow. "I believe I am expected."

"Don't keep his lordship standing there, Amanda," a sharp voice commanded. "Show him in."

The door opened wide and Pensley saw his hostess seated on the far side of the room. She was dressed in a brown silk dress that contrived to point up the unfashionable darkness of her skin. She had the look of one who has come from a warmer climate, and Pensley found himself silently conceding that in saying she had just returned from India, perhaps Mrs. Crowley was telling the truth.

"Please be seated, m'lord," she said in a creditably steady voice. "Amanda, you may leave us."

The woman did so without the least trace of reluctance. Wise creature, Pensley thought grimly as he took a seat on a sofa opposite Mrs. Crowley. For several long moments they regarded each other without speaking. At last Mrs. Crowley said, "Do you mean to tell me why you are here, m'lord?"

Pensley leaned back and crossed his arms against

his chest. "To discover why you are defaming Mrs. Lawford, Mrs. Crowley. If that is, indeed, your true name."

"Oh, it is, m'lord," she replied with a sharp look. "You shan't catch me out on that one. Mr. Crowley and I were wed, right and tight, here in England before ever we set out for India. Twelve years ago next October. Record right where it should be in the parish church, and I could show it to you anytime I wished. I should like to see Mrs. Lawford do the same."

"How do you know that she can not?" Pensley asked. "How do you know that she is not going to prove you to be the liar? I have heard the tale you have been spreading, that your husband was stationed near Mrs. Lawford's father and that you know, firsthand, there was no marriage to Hugo Lawford."

"That's right," Mrs. Crowley said, her jaw thrust forward.

"Indeed? Then no doubt you have the record to prove it," Pensley demanded.

"Record?" Mrs. Crowley was indignant. "To prove that woman never married Mr. Lawford? How could I have?"

With a dangerously quiet voice Pensley replied, "I meant record to prove where your husband was, or perhaps still is, stationed. Where is your husband, Mrs. Crowley?"

The lady gripped her two hands together in her lap as she replied, "That's not your affair, I should think."

"On the contrary," Pensley said harshly, "if you don't tell me, I shall make it my business to know."

Again, for several moments there was silence as

Mrs. Crowley stared at him. At last she took a deep breath and said, "Very well. I warned him there might be difficulties, that someone might ask my history, and there it is. My husband is a captain in the East India Company and is stationed now in Kanpur not far from where *she* was living with her family in India." Mrs. Crowley paused and said a trifle defensively, "You can check that if you like."

"And your husband. His reasons for not returning to England with you?" Pensley persisted. "Or, perhaps, yours for returning to England without him?"

Mrs. Crowley glared at Lord Pensley with patent dislike. "I shan't answer, m'lord."

Slowly, gracefully, Richard rose to his feet. "What a pity," he drawled. "Now I shall have to go to great lengths to discover the reasons myself. And when I have, I shall have to find you and publicize those reasons to everyone about you."

"Sit down, m'lord," she said hastily. When he had, she added darkly, "I shouldn't have thought a gentleman like yourself would stoop to such things." She paused hopefully, but Pensley merely inclined his head, a half-smile upon his face, and she went on, "Very well. I'll tell you. When I married George, everyone said I had married beneath me. But I wouldn't believe it then. Now I do. Twelve years, almost, we've been married. Comfortable years. And if there was a marked cooling of George's affections a few years back, well, I am sure it is no more than could be said of most marriages. I wasn't entirely a green girl when I married him. I knew he'd been accounted a wild one by nearly everyone who knew him. But I knew he'd settle down out in India. And so he did. Tolerably well. For a good long time. But then, a few years after the uprising in '06, he took it into his head that as a companyman it might be wise to get to know some of the natives. Keep an ear to the ground. That sort of thing. And who knows but what he wasn't right."

She paused and Pensley nodded encouragingly. After a moment Mrs. Crowley went on, a note of bitterness entering her voice as she said, "If that's what he was doing, that is. Anyway, for a long time things went along quite well. George's commanding officer even commended him upon his initiative. Then, just about a year ago, things changed. George brought home a native girl and set her up in the *bibi-gurh* behind our bungalow. I didn't say anything at first, because of course there were other men like George who set up native girls in those little houses. And it wasn't the first time he had sought diversion with other women."

"But never virtually within your own house before, I should wager," Pensley said gently.

Mrs. Crowley forgot herself so far as to throw him a grateful look. "Yes, you're right about that. And even in India it was a bit much. But then, then things became truly impossible. George told me that he was bringing the girl right into the bungalow and that if I didn't like it I could leave. In fact, that I should leave anyway. He gave me enough funds for my passage back to England and then said he would be quit of me and I was to be on my own."

Pensley observed the ashen whiteness of Mrs. Crowley's face and found he could not blame her for her distress. "Why didn't you go to your husband's commanding officer?" he asked, puzzled. "Surely he could have compelled your husband not to treat you in such a manner."

"So he would have." Mrs. Crowley nodded as she

spoke. "But I couldn't do so. George would simply have run away with the girl. He said he would, and I believe he meant it. I would have been left alone there and everyone would have known what had occurred. No, I chose instead to salvage my pride by leaving at once, before anyone knew what he had done, and so that it would be said he brought the girl into the house only after I had left."

"Except that by the time you arrived in England you realized that pride was a poor substitute for something to live on. Scarcely a way to feed and clothe and house yourself," Pensley suggested curtly.

"Yes," she answered a trifle defiantly. "I knew I should have to look for some sort of position. Perhaps as a governess or companion or something, and I found I couldn't bear it."

"So when a gentleman came to you and offered you a great deal of money to spread a false tale about Hugo Lawford's widow you accepted," Pensley suggested politely.

Mrs. Crowley looked down at her hands. "I didn't know it was a lie, did I? No one at Kanpur knew what the truth was about that marriage. Everything was at sixes and sevens with cholera at the time. *He* said she was a fraud, that *he* could prove it, given time, but he hoped to save himself the time and trouble by scaring her off now. That's why I did it, because I believed him."

"And after you had seen Mrs. Lawford? Even at a distance you must have known she was telling the truth," Pensley said harshly. Mrs. Crowley didn't answer and he said, biting off the words, "By then you couldn't bear to give it up, could you? The money, the companion he supplied to keep an eye on you? The respectability?"

"You're wrong about Amanda," Mrs. Crowley said, meeting Pensley's eyes. "He didn't supply *her*. She was an old school friend who'd fallen on times just as hard as my own. Since I could, I decided to share my good fortune with her. I'm not quite as heartless as you seem to make out."

Still seated, Pensley managed a half-bow. "My apologies," he said bitingly.

Stung, she retorted, "You sit there so smugly, m'lord, judging me. But you've never had to face a life without funds, have you? You've never wondered where the money would come from to feed yourself, have you? Or pay for a place to sleep? You've never had to face the pity of a hundred faces because your husband chose a dancing girl over you. You've never known what it is like to be without money or position or simple respect, have you, m'lord? Do you know how many acquaintances suddenly forget who you are when you have no money? Or how many relatives delight in saying that having made one's bed one must lie in it? You've never lived a day in your life when you haven't known your needs were taken care of, or I think you might be a little kinder."

When at last Pensley answered, he spoke quietly. Nevertheless he did not give ground. "How much were you paid?" he demanded.

"One thousand pounds," Mrs. Crowley said evenly. "Not a princely sum to you, I expect. But to me it means a great deal."

"I'll double it if you tell me who paid you and if you agree to undo the damage you've done," Pensley replied.

Mrs. Crowley laughed harshly. "P'rhaps I should speak to *him* first. It may be he would double *your* offer."

"I doubt it," Richard said curtly. "If it is the man I think, then his situation is desperate and those funds he did pay you with must have been borrowed. Moreover, even if he could pay you, I should still be here, knowing the truth about you, and I should make it my business to see that the rest of the *ton* did as well. Now tell me: who paid you and will you repair the damage you've done to Mrs. Lawford?"

Mrs. Crowley rose to her feet and began to pace the room. "I haven't much choice, have I?" she said. Pensley shook his head and she turned to face him. "Very well. It was a Julian Lawford who paid me. Not that he ever told me his real name. No, it was always Mr. Jennings, but I've seen him at various places since, often enough to know he's really Mr. Lawford. But how you expect me to be able to help Mrs. Lawford is beyond me. If I try to tell everyone I was mistaken, they'll only think I've been bought off, and that won't do either of us any good."

"Very true," Pensley conceded. "And I don't ask that you do. The only person I wish you to tell the entire story to is Mr. Nicholson. Indeed, I shall expect you to write out such a signed statement for him. But as for the *ton*, here is what I wish you to do. . . ."

19

"We'll make home in half a day less, I shouldn't wonder," Annie observed with some satisfaction.

Drusilla looked out the window at the countryside they were passing through as she said dryly, "Or we should if I had chosen to travel by the major roads. These are not so good as those we used when we went to London, but at least they are free of snow."

It was on the tip of Annie's tongue to ask if her mistress regretted leaving London. Or even to express sympathy with the impulse that had led Mrs. Lawford to choose a route upon which they would be most unlikely to encounter members of the *ton*. But she did not. Instead, she observed with a grateful sigh, "Your late husband, ma'am, didn't pinch pennies on his coach or his horses, the Lord be praised."

Drusilla smiled. "No, he didn't. Compared with the native *gharries* I became accustomed to in India this is scandalously well-sprung!"

These pleasant reflections, however, were abruptly brought to an end. It was midafternoon and they were not yet clear of the Chiltern hills when Drusilla felt the carriage lurch and then overturn. Only the skill of Hugo's coachman kept the crash from being far worse, for he had at the last moment realized something was amiss and had slowed the horses as far as possible. But when Drusilla and Annie clambered down, they found the situation far from good. One wheel of the coach lay shattered by the side of the road, there had been damage to the underbelly of the coach, and the horses pranced nervously within their traces. Boxes and trunks lay scattered everywhere and the groom appeared slightly stunned.

Prosaically Annie brushed the hem of her skirt where it had acquired some dust when she had gotten out of the carriage. "I think, ma'am, we shall not be reaching Lawford Manor so early, after all."

With a wry smile Drusilla agreed. "Quite right, Annie. Indeed, I fear we shall be fortunate if we are not forced to walk as far as the nearest town."

At this the coachman who had been occupied in quieting the horses was shocked into replying, "You cannot, ma'am! As soon as Tom recovers, it's him we'll be sending to find an inn where a carriage can be fetched to come and get you. And it's hoping he won't have to go all the way to Wallingford, I am. If I thought that, I should have to send him back to Nettlebed, and that I'm not wanting to do."

Drusilla looked around her at the deserted road and reflected upon the villages they had passed. "There ought to be an inn ahead, though I shouldn't be surprised," she said at last, "if we find that a horse cart is the best they can manage. Well, no matter. So long as we aren't hurt we shall contrive something. Or is anyone hurt? Tom?"

The groom, who had been sitting by the side of the road, now stood, rubbing his head. "I'll be meself in a moment, ma'am," he said. Then, to the coachman, "Shall I hold the horses?"

"Aye. I want a look at the carriage."

"Rogers, are you hurt?" Drusilla asked her coachman.

Impatiently he shrugged. "Nothing hurt but my pride, ma'am. I can't think how I came to overturn us. That's why I want to be looking at the wheel and shaft and such."

"Annie?" Drusilla turned to her maid.

Annie hesitated, her lower lip caught between her teeth. Then she said matter-of-factly, "Just as well we needn't walk, ma'am. I seem to have somehow hurt my ankle when we overturned." Then, noting her employer's expression, she added, "And it's nothing to fret about. I shall be right as a trivet in no time. What about yourself, ma'am?"

Drusilla took a moment to consider the question. A trifle ruefully she said, "I am quite unharmed. Save for *my* pride. Perhaps we should have taken the main road, after all."

But Rogers would have none of that. Sternly he said, "Now as to that, ma'am, I wouldn't agree. If we had, we would have overturned far sooner, I'm thinking."

Startled, both Annie and Drusilla looked at the coachman. "I think you'd best explain what you mean," Drusilla said.

Rogers hesitated. Reluctantly he grumbled, "I oughtn't to have said anything."

"But you did," Drusilla pointed out implacably, "and I wish to know what you meant."

Still grumbling, the coachman replied, "Seems someone tampered with the coach. There's no way that wheel would have come off by itself. Not like that. Meant to come off in these hills I'd guess. Which we would of hit sooner if we'd taken the main road," he concluded severely.

"I see." Drusilla's expression was strained and white. "But we would at least have found a town large enough to boast a competent carriage smith on the main road."

"Oh, aye, and been easy to find ourselves if anyone wanted to see the success of their handiwork," Annie pointed out dryly.

"Or wished to finish it," Tom added with relish.

"That'll be quite enough," Rogers said stonily. "I oughtn't to have said a word, ma'am, but I thought perhaps you'd best know."

"Oh, yes, forewarned is forearmed," Drusilla agreed. "I just had not thought anyone disliked me enough to do this."

"Envied might be the better word," Annie grumbled. Then, more briskly she said to Rogers, "Well, at any rate, talking won't pay the toll. Tom had best be on his way to find some means of getting us to an inn and finding a carriage smith."

Sometime later, Tom returned driving a small pony cart. He was accompanied by a burly fellow who introduced himself at once. "I be the blacksmith, mum. Aye, and repair what few carts and carriages folks have hereabouts. We're not on the main road, though, and most of my work is with horses that have cast a shoe. Though you're not the first to turn over here."

"Well, you'd best come and have a look at this wheel, then," Rogers said to the man. To Tom he added, "Have you found an inn for Mrs. Lawford?"

"Aye," Tom nodded hastily. "I bespoke rooms for you, ma'am, at the Four Ducks."

The blacksmith added over his shoulder, "I don't think it's not what you're accustomed to, ma'am, but it's all we have hereabouts. You'll find it a clean place and the Wilkins eager to please." He paused, then added shrewdly, "You needn't worry about arriving so unceremoniously. Most of the business the Wilkins do is because of carriages that take this road too fast."

"Yes, well, I shall be satisfied so long as it has a roof," Drusilla retorted. "Come, Annie, there's room for us both in the cart and for one or two of our bandboxes."

There was actually room for a little more than that, and both Annie and her mistress were relieved to see that they would have at least one change of clothing with them right from the start.

It was half an hour's ride to the inn and Drusilla found it just as the blacksmith had described: small but snug, and the proprietor and his wife eager to please. "We've not got a private parlor, ma'am," Mrs. Wilkins said anxiously, "but there's nobody in the coffeeroom now, and if you would step inside, you'll find it warm and I can have tea laid for you in no time."

"Thank you," Drusilla replied. "I should also like to go up to my room, but first we'd best take care of your ankle, Annie. If you could send someone to fetch a doctor, Mrs. Wilkins, I should be grateful. My maid has injured her ankle."

"That would be Dr. Hathaway," Mr. Wilkins said doubtfully, "but he's been called away for a few days. Dunno who else to send for. P'rhaps the midwife?"

Abruptly Drusilla shook her head. "No, I shall attend to it myself, then."

"But it wouldn't be fitting!" Annie and the Wilkins all managed to gasp at the same moment. "I could send the boy into Wallingford. They are accustomed there to being called upon when carriages overturn hereabouts."

"Perhaps that would be best," Drusilla agreed. "I know what I am about. We did not always have a doctor to hand in India, either. And even before that, in Yorkshire, with three brothers I assure you I saw a good many sprains. But I should not like to risk the injury being worse. Send your boy and I shall do no more now than to make Annie comfortable."

Recognizing the determined glint in her mistress's eye, Annie did not argue further but followed Mrs. Lawford into the coffeeroom. "I warn you, you shall have to rest the foot," Drusilla said sternly. "Fortunately Mrs. Wilkins seems a good sort and will oblige."

A few minutes and Drusilla had contrived to bind the ankle and set cold compresses on the injured portion. Then she followed Mrs. Wilkins upstairs to her room, where she gratefully laid aside her own bonnet and pelisse and changed from half-boots to indoor slippers.

She had just descended the stairs when Rogers was shown into the parlor. Turning his hat in his hand, he said, "Bad news, ma'am. They've not got another wheel hereabouts to fit the coach. We'll be needing to send to Wallingford for someone to come and repair the coach. The smith is a good man, but the shaft is ruint as well and he's not willing to trust that he'd catch whatever else might be wrong."

"I see," Drusilla said quietly.

"We might hire a post and four from there, as well, to take you home. Or back to London. Tom and I could follow with the carriage when it's repaired," he added anxiously.

Drusilla hesitated. She looked at Annie, whose white, strained face bespoke the extent of her injury. She made up her mind. Decisively Drusilla shook her head and said, "No, Rogers. I am content to wait here until the coach—and Annie's ankle—should heal."

"Very well, ma'am," Rogers replied. He hesitated. Drusilla opened her purse and gave him some guineas. "Here. This should cover the cost of repairs. If it does not, come and let me know."

Once more Rogers nodded, the grim expression still upon his face. "I'm thinking, ma'am," he said hesitantly, "that perhaps we ought to remove to Wallingford ourselves. Not today, o'course, but mayhap tomorrow when Miss Annie's ankle will be better."

"I shall think about it," was all Drusilla would say.

Yet again Rogers nodded, then he left. It seemed to Drusilla she could hear him muttering as he went, "This ain't what I'm accustomed to. Cutting through shafts and loosening spokes on wheels. No, nor I don't like this at all!"

Annie waited until he was gone and then she spoke to her mistress. "You might have gone ahead without me, ma'am. I could well have returned with Rogers."

With a shake of her head and a smile Drusilla replied, "No, Annie. But you need not fret. I have already told you I am quite content to remain here even if it should be a week or more. Or to remove all of us to Wallingford, if the doctor should allow it, and wait there for the carriage to be repaired."

At that moment Mrs. Wilkins bustled in with a tidy

tea tray for the two women. Only when everything was set out to her satisfaction did she curtsy and leave. As they ate, Annie forced herself to say, "Oughtn't we to send word to the manor, ma'am, that we've been delayed upon the road?"

Drusilla considered the matter. After a moment she shook her head and said, "I think not. They will wonder but decide, no doubt, that we turned back to London. And in London . . ." She stopped. "In London, I think I should prefer that whoever tampered with the carriage should believe that their scheme has worked."

Annie shivered. "Aye. I shouldn't want whoever it was to come looking to finish the job."

Drusilla nodded soberly. "That's why I don't want anyone to know where to find us," she said.

After tea, Drusilla went up to her room to rest, blissfully unaware of the plans her servants and Mrs. Wilkins were about to hatch. It was fortunate that she had no notion what was intended, for she would surely have objected. As it was, by the time she discovered their intentions, it was too late to do so. "Which was," Annie later informed her sternly, "only right and proper."

20

In his study, Lord Pensley stared across the desk at his visitor, Julian Lawford. "But my dear fellow, how can I possibly help you?"

"By telling me how you persuaded Mrs. Crowley to repeat such slanderous lies about me," Julian replied affably.

"Lies? Mrs. Crowley?" Pensley asked with mock astonishment. "But I thought her integrity beyond question. Certainly everyone held it so when she claimed Mrs. Lawford was not Hugo's widow."

"I never said so," Julian pointed out.

"Ah, but then you had no need to," Pensley replied in dulcet tones. "Your cleverness was quite an inspiration, I must say."

"Be careful you do not live to regret this," Julian said silkily.

Pensley raised his eyebrows in surprise. "Regret that Mrs. Crowley so far forgot herself as to allow everyone to know she is well-acquainted with you, Mr., er, Jennings? What has that to do with me? Though I must say I was gratified to learn that you have such a generous nature. One thousand pounds, indeed! What a handsome sum to bestow upon the poor, destitute woman. And how kind in her to acknowledge your generosity."

For the first time since he had entered the room Julian Lawford showed signs of losing his temper. "It is a great pity that dueling has gone out of fashion," he said with clenched teeth. "Otherwise, I should take great pleasure in running you through with a sword or shooting you between the eyes."

It was Pensley's turn to grin affably. "Oh, I shouldn't think so," he replied. "We have both shot at Manton's, you know, and I have a far better aim. As for the sword," Pensley paused to cough deprecatingly, "I have seen you fence."

With an effort Julian forced himself to smile as well. "Perhaps you are right, though I shouldn't like to think so. Nevertheless I am not done yet, Pensley. Mrs. Crowley leaves London tonight and I shall burn the letter."

"Letter?" Richard asked innocently.

Julian sighed. "Really, Pensley, this is becoming tedious. The letter. I am quite certain you have seen it. It is a forgery, I don't doubt, but a clever one. I should not want Mrs. Crowley to show it about. So, Mrs. Crowley leaves London tonight." He paused as though considering whether or not to ask his next question. In the end he did. "I don't suppose you can tell me whether Nicholson saw that letter? And if he did, whether *he* was clever enough to realize it was a forgery."

Pensley smiled. "Let us say he saw a similar letter. A genuine letter. That, in fact, Mrs. Crowley's letter was a copy of the other."

Julian closed his eyes. "Do you know, Pensley," he said conversationally, "there are times when I quite hate you?"

"How nice to know we feel the same about each

other," Richard retorted, still smiling. "What will you do now?"

"Oh, a retreat from London, no doubt," Julian replied, opening his eyes again. "But not at once. One would not like to be seen running away. Besides, I await certain news."

"News?" Richard asked sharply.

"Mrs. Lawford's direction," Julian said innocently. "I should like to be able to write her and congratulate her upon her good fortune." As Richard watched him warily, Julian went on, "I thought, you see, that Mrs. Lawford had returned to Hugo's home. The one near you, in fact. But that appears not to be the case. Perhaps you can tell me where she is."

Frowning, Richard ignored the question. "How do you know she has not returned to Lawford Manor?" he demanded.

Julian stood up. "Because," he said blandly, "I sent a note there and received no reply. Moreover, the groom who took the message said that though she had been expected, Mrs. Lawford never arrived."

Pensley rose to his full height. "Let us be certain we understand each other," he said slowly. "Did you, in fact, expect Mrs. Lawford to be somehow delayed? Or to alter her plans?"

Again Julian spread his hands. "I merely felt concern because she seemed in such a distressed state when she made the decision to leave London. Indeed, she did not even tell us she intended to return to Lawford Manor. I discovered *that* only through my servants, who were, it seems, on excellent terms with Mrs. Lawford's maid. Ah, well, perhaps she simply altered her plans," he ended brightly.

"Perhaps," Pensley said grimly. "For your sake, I hope that is true."

Julian raised an eyebrow. "Indeed? But we have already agreed that dueling is no longer *bon ton*."

"There are other avenues open to me," Pensley answered mildly. "You have said a great many things to me this afternoon that a magistrate would find most interesting."

"But, my dear fellow, there would be only your word against mine," Julian said in protest. "Particularly as I should be obliged to tell the magistrate that it was not the cruel gossip about Mrs. Lawford that drove her from London but your unwanted attentions."

"What?" Pensley demanded incredulously.

"Why, everyone knows you had, indeed still have, right of refusal over whom Mrs. Lawford may marry. It is little known, however, that she confided in my mother and myself that you were pressing her to marry you, saying that otherwise you should never give your approval to her remarriage. It was to escape your persecution that she fled London," Julian said, meeting Pensley's eyes coolly.

"That is untrue," Pensley retorted.

Julian smiled. "Since we are alone, I am free to allow that you are correct. But in a court of law? Ah, that would be a far different matter. I should be obliged to use every means at my disposal to protect myself, and I fancy this story should go over very well. *Poor* Mrs. Lawford! And everyone knows how kind my mother and I have been to her."

Pensley sat down, his face once more calm. "Very clever," he agreed dryly. "How unfortunate for you, however, that there is a witness to what you have just said. Mr. Nicholson, I suggest you come back in now."

As Julian Lawford went ashen-white, the solicitor strolled through a door that Julian had not noticed before but that he now realized had been open the entire time. Mr. Nicholson regarded Julian with marked disapproval. "You have made a grave error," he told young Lawford sharply. "But then you have always had such a nature. It is precisely that which led your uncle, Hugo Lawford, to leave so much of his funds away from you. Mind you, I blame your mother greatly as well. You will be fortunate if you do not find yourself facing charges."

In dulcet tones Julian replied, "But for the moment at least, I do not. And so I shall bid the pair of you good day and take my leave."

Nicholson would have stopped him, but Pensley shook his head. "Let him go. So long as he does not know Mrs. Lawford's direction, there is no further mischief he can do."

Nicholson coughed. "As to that, m'lord, I would guess he has already begun to circulate that rumor. The nonsensical tale that you are the cause of Mrs. Lawford's flight from London." At Pensley's look of astonishment he added, "Julian Lawford's mother came to me, in strictest confidence, of course, to ask if there were any way to stop your persecution of Mrs. Lawford. I collect, from something another client said, that she has spoken not only to me but to several of her, er, bosom bows as well," Nicholson concluded impassively.

"Good God, what audacity," Pensley exclaimed.

"Quite so," Nicholson agreed. "Particularly as it is the sort of rumor that you cannot deny without appearing to give it even further credence." He paused, then added quietly, "It appears, m'lord, that Julian Lawford does not have his aunt's direction. May I inquire as to whether *you* know where she may be found?"

Pensley frowned. "You may inquire all you like, but the answer is that if she is not at Lawford Manor, where I believe she meant to go, I do not know where to look for her."

Noting the strained look on Pensley's face, Nicholson asked gently, "Do you fear that she has met with an, er, accident, m'lord?"

"I don't know what to fear," Pensley answered frankly. "You heard what he said. But Julian Lawford would have to be desperate to risk such a step." He paused, then added, "Hugo must have had windmills in his head, however, to state that Julian would inherit everything if Mrs. Lawford should die, unless she made direct provision otherwise."

"As to that," Nicholson said thoughtfully, "I believe Hugo Lawford considered his nephew capable of great mischief but not, er, that is, of nothing worse. Recollect also that he was suffering from cholera at the time and perhaps wondering if he was dealing altogether fairly with the boy. Nevertheless, directly we find Mrs. Lawford, I would suggest that we ask her to draw up a will herself, disposing of things should she die. She is a sensible young woman, I am certain she will agree. The greatest difficulty, I apprehend, is simply to find her. Have you any ideas where to look, m'lord?"

"None," Pensley answered curtly. "But I shall find her. And when I do, you shall come along to help us write the will on the spot! And to arrange for a copy to be hand-delivered to Julian Lawford and his mother."

"An excellent notion, m'lord," the solicitor agreed quietly. "By the by, given the letter from Amesley as well as the depositions taken from those native servants of Hugo's who could still be found and the commanding officer of the cantonment, I anticipate no further difficulties establishing the right of Mrs. Lawford's inheritance. Even without the letter his chief wallah held."

Nicholson paused. "I collect the fellow did not realize its importance, but when my agent spoke with him, he produced it upon the spot. There is no question that however shaky, it is Hugo Lawford's handwriting. And he leaves no doubt that he married Drusilla Crandall and why."

Pensley nodded grimly. "Yes, he felt he'd finally found a young woman with some sense. Also he had reason to feel that leaving Julian his wealth would be a disastrous deed. Even I didn't know, until I read that letter, that Julian had tried to reestablish the Hell-Fire Club. Hugo must have found out just before, or perhaps even after, he set sail for India. How fortunate," he went on, "that those inquiries you set in motion when Mrs. Lawford first appeared with Hugo Lawford's will should have resulted in such a satisfactory reply at precisely this time."

"Just so," Nicholson agreed, rubbing his hands together. "I fancy that enough members of the *ton* have seen our edited copy of Hugo Lawford's letter, omitting the portion concerning the Hell-Fire Club, that Mrs. Lawford need not fear ostracism the next time she is in London. Mrs. Crowley was most zealous in her efforts on our behalf."

Pensley looked at Nicholson and said quietly, "I was surprised to see the letter, you know. I was aware that you had made inquiries, of course, but I had no notion they were so far-reaching. You always appeared to accept Mrs. Lawford's claim with great equanimity."

Nicholson also raised his eyebrows. "I did," he replied. "As I have told you before, it seemed inconceivable, once I had met the lady, that she could have been guilty of attempting such a deception. But my position as solicitor and trustee of Hugo Lawford's estate required that I make such a search regardless of my personal feelings in the matter."

"Particularly as the other relatives in the case seemed certain to challenge her legitimacy?" Pensley hazarded with a smile.

"Let us simply say that I was indeed puzzled that they did not challenge with greater force at the time. But no doubt they thought Mrs. Lawford would be easy prey for young Julian's charms." He paused, then added hesitantly, "Particularly as certain legal matters touching on, er, moral issues dictated that it would be advantageous for Julian Lawford to acquire a wife as quickly as possible."

"But he has not," Pensley pointed out.

"No. Young Lawford did not pay sufficient attention to the provision that your consent was required to Mrs. Lawford's remarriage. Nor did he realize that she was in shock and not the pliant young girl everyone said she appeared to be," Nicholson said blandly.

"No, that she is not," Pensley agreed with a sharp laugh. "What do you think Julian will do once we have protected her by having *her* will written?"

"Flee the country, I shouldn't wonder," Nicholson

said with no little satisfaction. "There is, after all, a branch of the family in the Americas, and I shouldn't be surprised if Julian and his mother call on relatives there for a while."

"No," Pensley agreed, "on the other hand, I should also not be surprised if they come about here. In any event, our first priority must be to find Mrs. Lawford before Julian concludes that all his difficulties will be solved if she passes away at once."

Julian Lawford had no affairs more pressing than the need to find Drusilla Lawford before anyone else. The same might have been said of Lord Pensley. Both sent out runners to try to find word of where Drusilla had gone.

For someone who was determined, it was not really very difficult to find some trace of her. Her staff at Lawford Manor had received notice she would arrive. She did not. The main roads were checked for news of a carriage bearing her north-west or westward. Eventually an ostler was found at Henley-on-Thames who remembered her because of the generous way her coachman paid for trifling services rendered.

Both Pensley and Lawford meant to leave at the earliest possible moment to follow this lead. Julian Lawford, however, held an advantage. He knew that an accident might have been expected and where it was likely to occur. Therefore, he was the first to reach the Four Ducks. Mrs. Wilkins stoutly denied having had any such customers as he described, but not everyone in the area had been warned and Julian soon discovered that a carriage had overturned here-abouts.

With a shrug he continued on toward Wallingford.
A carriage had overturned and it might have been
Drusilla's. No doubt she had not much liked the sight
of the Four Ducks and had decided to wait in
Wallingford for her carriage to be repaired. Or
perhaps she had even been killed outright and that
was why Mrs. Wilkins had had no guests. *If* she had
had no guests. Of that Julian was not at all certain,
for he had met Mrs. Wilkins' sort before and they
always seemed to dislike him on sight. She might
have concealed anything.

Another man would have left the search to others,
but Julian Lawford was determined to find his aunt
before Lord Pensley. Therefore, he bowled into
Wallingford a short time later and immediately put
up at the town's largest inn, the Conqueror. Some
might have considered that imprudent, considering
his precarious financial position, but Julian could
not bear petty economics. That was why he had
counted so heavily upon Uncle Hugo's inheritance
and been so wild with rage when he discovered the
terms of Hugo's will. But with luck the nightmare
would soon be over. He meant to continue his search
at once, of course, but he was wise enough to realize
this would take somewhat longer than in Nettlebed.

If nothing else Wallingford was a riverside town
with considerably more commerce. Travelers
headed north to Oxford or south to Reading might
pass through here. It was, moreover, a town with a
strong sense of history and more than one tutor had
been known to bring his charges to the town to learn
that William the Conqueror had crossed the Thames
here in 1066 and Queen Maud had fled here from

Oxford Castle in 1142. Neatly built Georgian houses proclaimed prosperity, and it was evident that the town knew how to cater to the comfort of travelers. It would, Julian concluded, be an excellent base from which to discover his aunt's trail.

21

As Lord Pensley gave certain orders to the majordomo of his London establishment, Nicholson contented himself with muttering quietly, "Dear, dear, I do hope we find her quickly. I understand the importance of my availability to write her will, but to be gone from London for some time is not a thing I can like."

"You do so often enough for other clients," Pensley broke in heartlessly.

"Yes, but then I know how long I shall be gone and when I will return," Nicholson countered. "Mind you, I am not suggesting I do not come along, I am merely pointing out the difficulty for my staff."

"They will contrive admirably without you, I am sure," Lady Ratherby said. At Nicholson's sharp look she continued in dulcet tones, "After all, you have trained them so well."

"Quite."

A trifle impatiently Pensley turned to his sister and said, "Are you sure you ought to be coming with us, Cordelia? I mean to travel fast and light and I cannot think the journey will be a comfortable one for any of us."

Lady Ratherby, who lacked her brother's inches, stared up at him and smiled. "You need not fret about me, Richard, I've no intention of throwing a rub in your way. But I will not be put off the first adventure that has offered itself in years." She paused, then added briskly, "Besides, if Julian Lawford did somehow contrive an accident, perhaps I may be of help. As the mother of several children you may believe me when I say that I know what to do by a sickbed."

"Very well," Pensley agreed curtly, "then let us be off. I have had word she was seen at Henley-on-Thames and headed northwestward from there."

"That is not very far," Nicholson observed disapprovingly. "Scarcely halfway to Oxford."

"True, but at least we know the road she took," Pensley replied, "and that is something. Should you prefer that we waited until my man should discover more? I do not. We know that Julian Lawford is also on her trail and I should not like him to meet up with her first."

Lady Ratherby shuddered. "I have never particularly liked young Julian, but of late he begins to frighten me. One would almost think he has taken women in dislike."

"Except his mother," Pensley added. "No doubt she would have gone with him to find Mrs. Lawford were it not more important for her to be in London to scotch sordid rumors."

Mrs. Drusilla Lawford had quickly abandoned Wallingford, realizing at once that it was far too public a town for her needs. And yet she had not wished to remove far, nor had she wished to draw attention to herself by asking about the nearby towns. In the end she chose Ewelme because it was close and she had heard of it and few travelers would be likely to linger there, though such a thing would not be unknown. In short, a small town, yet one of sufficient interest that the rare historical visitor would not be remarked upon too greatly.

Mrs. Lawford did not speak of her plans publicly, of course. Instead, as she paid her shot at the Sword and Arrow, Mrs. Lawford let it be known that now that her carriage had been satisfactorily seen to, she meant to continue her journey homeward. No mention was made, however, of Lawford Manor nor the nearby village of Cropthorne. Instead, a listener might have developed the mistaken impression Mrs. Lawford lived somewhere close to Warwick.

The innkeeper hastened to assist Mrs. Lawford to her carriage, for it was evident that she had recently injured her ankle. Mrs. Lawford's maid also rendered her assistance and soon the party was settled and ready to leave.

Inside the carriage Mrs. Lawford turned to her maid and said coolly as they jostled along, "I think that went rather well, Annie. A pity you have such a pretty face, but I will allow you have done a remarkable job of effacing yourself."

The maid laughed. "And you of acquiring countenance, Mrs. Lawford," she retorted amiably. "One would think you were to the manner born."

"On the contrary, I am the daughter of a simple person," Mrs. Lawford countered.

"You are also remarkably pretty when you choose to be," her maid observed dryly. "I begin to see why Rogers was so eager to assist you when you were injured."

Mrs. Lawford straightened, a pleased look upon her face. "Well, I do not think I can pass for twenty, but we have contrived well enough. *You* certainly might pass for thirty."

"How kind of you to remind me what an antidote I must now appear," her maid laughed. She paused, then said soberly, "Truly, I am still not easy in my mind that we have changed places."

"Don't trust me to pass myself off as a lady?" Mrs. Lawford asked. "Or is it you don't like working for your living?"

The maid shook her head. "Neither. And, indeed, you have made good use of the years you've worked in *ton*-ish homes. It is extraordinary how convincing a Mrs. Lawford you make. No, I'm more afraid of danger to you if the person who tampered with the carriage follows us."

Mrs. Lawford sniffed. "That's why Rogers and Mrs. Wilkins and Tom and I made up the plan between ourselves and set it about that you were the maid and I the mistress. So you couldn't object. And it has answered, hasn't it? Anyone looking for our traveling party by description will be thrown off. And that will be safer for all of us."

"In short, I had best become accustomed to looking an antidote." The maid grinned.

"Better an antidote, *Annie*, than a corpse," Mrs. Lawford retorted tartly.

"To be sure," the maid agreed cordially. "I wonder what Julian Lawford will make of it if he crosses our trail himself?"

"That I hope we shall not find out," Mrs. Lawford replied with a shudder. "It is to be hoped he will think he has mistaken us for another party named Lawford but if not that we are somehow on our way to Warwick. I prefer that we should turn our minds to Ewelme. What do you know of it? Other than that it is nearby and we may reach it without undue jostling to my poor ankle?"

The maid smiled. "It is in its own way rather famous. The granddaughter of Chaucer lived there as the Duchess of Suffolk and established, I understand, a good many almshouses, a hospital, and a school. And there is, of course, a church."

"You seem to be remarkably well-informed," Mrs. Lawford sniffed. "It is to be hoped that you will not be recognized from former visits there."

"Oh, but I shan't be," the maid was quick to protest, "for I've never actually seen it. My father was fond of telling me about good works that women had done, hoping I might someday follow in their footsteps, I suppose. The story of Alice, the duchess, particularly pleased him."

"Very well," Mrs. Lawford said grandly. "Just so long as you do not forget yourself and behave impertinently, we shall manage quite well, I expect."

And with that both women dissolved into helpless laughter.

Julian Lawford was not laughing. He had expended a great deal of energy, time, and even money in trying to discover Drusilla's whereabouts. By the end of her first week in Ewelme he had already driven north to Warwick, cast about there for her trail, and finally returned to Wallingford convinced the news about Warwick had all been a hum. Had so much not been at stake he would have washed his hands of the whole matter. As it was, he once more put up at the Conqueror and sent his man out to make inquiries.

In the end it was a small thing that put him on the

road to Ewelme. A certain young doctor had attended Mrs. Lawford and been smitten with her maid. Thus he had paid careful attention when he saw her mistress's carriage take the road toward Watlington. And the only reason he had been in a position to see *that* was a call he had made upon a family in Shillingford. Fortune had so far smiled upon the fellow that he was able to think of cases that needed attending to in the nearby villages the very next day. And after that it was simple for, having found Mrs. Lawford, he attended her.

Julian Lawford felt grimly triumphant the day he discovered that intelligence. His man had failed to learn the name of the village where Mrs. Lawford was staying, but Dr. Allenby would know it. Julian made plans to set out at once to see him and then visit Mrs. Lawford before she should have a chance to move again.

He was, it is true, somewhat disturbed at the reported description of the traveling party. Either someone was a poor judge of women's ages or this was not Drusilla he was following. But whatever the truth, Julian was determined to know by nightfall. If it was not, he could return to London and begin to cast about again for her trail. If it was Drusilla, an accident would speedily be contrived and to the devil with the consequences. One way or the other, Julian was determined to be quit of this Oxfordshire valley he had begun to despise.

So he paid a call upon Allenby. When the doctor learned that Julian Lawford was a close relative as well as a dear friend of Mrs. Lawford, he was all eagerness to be of assistance and able to reassure Julian that he would still find the party in Ewelme.

* * *

Lady Ratherby spent much of that same week comfortably ensconced in Wallingford at the Ox and Mare, a more discreet establishment than the Conqueror, while her brother and Nicholson went dashing off to Warwick and back. She had very quickly decided that either they were following the wrong party—quite likely given the description of this Mrs. Lawford—or Drusilla had somehow gone to ground and was trying to throw off anyone in pursuit. If that were the case, Warwick was certain to yield nothing.

So Cordelia placidly waited in Wallingford, visiting certain families who were most flattered to welcome her and listening to the gossip of the inn as well as that of her peers. She was not surprised to hear about a young doctor who had been smitten with desire for a lady's maid traveling northwest from Wallingford. A lady whose carriage had overturned on the road from Nettlebed. She also discovered, women's gossip being more thorough than men's, that the maid's mistress had decided to break her journey in Ewelme and that the doctor contrived to call upon her almost every day. At that point Cordelia decided to go there as well.

And so, the next morning, Lady Ratherby left a message with the clerk of the Ox and Mare that she had decided to visit the church of St. Mary the Virgin in Ewelme. Then she climbed into the post chaise that had been hired for her convenience. She made one more stop, observing to the fellow who then joined her in the post chaise that it was always more comfortable to travel with a man.

22

Lady Ratherby, despite her stated intentions, did not immediately drive round to the church of St. Mary the Virgin in Ewelme. Instead, once she and her male companion reached the flint and brick village, they paused to partake of a light refreshment at the Five Feathers. There the innkeeper's wife was most obliging when asked about the attractions one ought to see in that town. "Nor you won't find yourself the only visitor we have," the woman added proudly. "Aside from two young gentlemen and their tutors making a historical tour of England, there be a nabob's widow come to see the sights. Not that she be going about much. Injured her ankle not a good many days past."

Cordelia frowned, not pleased to find how easy it was to discover Drusilla's whereabouts. "A nabob's widow? How extraordinary," she repeated as lightly as she was able. "I wonder if it may be the same widow I am acquainted with. May I ask where she is putting up?"

The innkeeper's wife tightened her lips in disapproval. "At the Boarshead. And it's not a place I could like even saving that we've scarcely enough custom, hereabouts, for two inns."

More alarmed than ever, Lady Ratherby directed

her coachman to go straight to the Boarshead. Only when she crossed the threshold and saw for herself that it was a respectable place did she cease to worry. At once the innkeeper of this establishment came forward. With deference but not servility, Cordelia was pleased to see, he asked, "May I help you? A bite to eat, p'rhaps? A nice, clean room, the sheets well-aired and the bed warmed at night, p'rhaps?"

Lady Ratherby smiled her most charming smile, the one few people could resist. "Thank you, but I believe a friend of mine may be staying here. Mrs. Lawford?"

At once the innkeeper nodded. "Aye, she is. If you would care to step into the parlor across the way, I make no doubt you'll find her in there. Poor lady, she can't go much about. An injured ankle, you see."

"Lead the way, please," Cordelia replied quickly. Then, to her companion she said, "Please wait for me out here, Mr. Stockley. If you are needed, I shall come fetch you."

"Very good, m'lady," was the fellow's excellent reply.

The innkeeper did as he was bid, and it was only a few moments later that he opened the door to the private parlor and said to the woman sitting there, her back to the door, "I've brought yo a visitor, ma'am, one I make no doubt you will be happy to see."

The woman turned at once, startled, it seemed, by the innkeeper's voice. Lady Ratherby waited until the door closed behind her, then she went forward and smiled as she said, "I'm so sorry, I appear to have made a dreadful mistake. The innkeeper said you were Mrs. Lawford and I had been told you were a nabob's widow and I thought perhaps you were someone I knew."

"Indeed?" the woman asked frostily. "And who may you be?"

Cordelia took a seat opposite the woman. "I am Lady Ratherby," she said. "My husband is Lord Ratherby, my brother is Lord Pensley. I daresay you don't know any of us and wish I would go to the devil and leave you be. It is just that I do know a Mrs. Lawford and she is the widow of a nabob and the coincidence seems extraordinary."

She stopped, aware that her words had had an astonishing effect on the other woman. "Is Lord Pensley here as well?" she demanded.

"Are you acquainted with my brother?" Lady Ratherby demanded, taken aback.

"No, but I am," came a voice from behind them.

Startled, Cordelia turned in time to see a lady's maid gently close the door and come forward. "Don't you recognize me?" she demanded with a soft laugh.

Lady Ratherby was about to deny it when suddenly she said, aghast, "Drusilla?"

Again the woman laughed. "Annie, at the moment. It seemed safer that way. Or so my loyal servants convinced me. We exchanged places shortly after a wheel came off our traveling coach and Rogers told me it was not an accident. It has answered extremely well, thus far. Everyone defers to Annie and pays scarcely any mind to me."

"Except Dr. Allenby," Cordelia observed.

"Is that how you found us?" Drusilla asked. "I had wondered."

"Well, there was more to it than that," Cordelia explained. "Someone remembered you at Henley-on-Thames. That told us what roads you were likely to have taken. The trail led to Wallingford and from there my brother and Mr. Nicholson have gone haring off to Warwick. I rather doubted that tale, however, and I stayed behind. It was not difficult to discover you might have gone to ground in Ewelme since Dr. Allenby has not troubled to hide his passion for Mrs. Lawford's maid. Then, once here, everyone was eager to tell me about the nabob's widow who had come to see the sights."

"Oh, dear," Drusilla said ruefully as she sat down. "And I thought we had been so clever. I don't suppose you know if Julian Lawford is on my trail as well?"

"He is," Cordelia confirmed promptly. "And what you will do about it, I cannot say. Richard is of the opinion that if you make your own will, one that leaves everything away from young Julian, he will cease to trouble you. For as it stands, if you die, he inherits."

"I see," Drusilla said thoughtfully. "Yes, that makes sense. And had I not been so distressed I must have thought of that myself. When do your brother and Nicholson return to Wallingford?"

Cordelia spread her hands helplessly. "I haven't the faintest notion," she said. "They left for Warwick three days ago."

Drusilla rested her chin in her hands as she considered the matter. "I cannot wait for their return," she said at last. "For if you have found us so easily, Julian may as well. No, it would be a good notion for me to write such a will right away and place a copy in the care of the local churchman so that even should Julian succeed in destroying the original, there will be one he cannot find."

"Oh, and I suppose that will resolve everything?" Annie/Mrs. Lawford demanded tartly.

With a sigh Drusilla replied, "No. But it is the best I can contrive upon the spur of the moment. Lady Ratherby, perhaps you had best go and ask the innkeeper where the nearest solicitor may be found."

"Lady Ratherby?" she asked with raised eyebrows. "I thought it was to be Drusilla and Cordelia between us."

"But, m'lady, that would scarcely be proper for a maid," Drusilla retorted in shocked accents. More seriously she added, "If I am careless of my role in private, I am likely to make an error in public."

With a laugh Cordelia rose. "Very well, I shall go and fetch a solicitor." She paused, a twinkle in her eyes as she said, "But I shan't trouble the proprietor of this establishment. I thought, you see, that a solicitor might be helpful to have and so I brought one from Wallingford with me. He is in the taproom right now, refreshing himself."

Drusilla blinked and then rushed over to impulsively embrace Cordelia. "You are a treasure," she said.

Mr. Stockley was quickly fetched and professed himself prepared to draw up the necessary papers immediately.

"I am afraid you have been put to a great deal of trouble," Drusilla told him, hesitantly.

Mr. Stockley looked startled at being addressed by a young woman who was clearly a lady's maid. His manners were impeccable, however, and so he cleared his throat and said, "Well, as to that, ma'am, Lady Ratherby has been quite generous in purchasing my services for the entire day. But I do confess myself to be a trifle bewildered. For which of you ladies am I to draw up such a document?"

"For me," Drusilla answered with a smile. "I know it must all seem very strange and not in the least *comme-il-faut*, but I am Mrs. Lawford and this is my maid Annie. We have exchanged places for the same reason I require your services. My late husband's nephew stands to inherit everything he left me if I should die intestate, and he has become impatient to do so."

"Good God," Mr. Stockley exclaimed. "I am appalled, utterly appalled! But surely you have called in the law?"

Drusilla shook her head. "I have no proof, only an accident to my carriage caused unmistakably by someone tampering with the wheel and the shaft. No, I have not gone to the law and I confess I am hoping that the mere existence, in several copies, of my will leaving everything to someone else will suffice to deter my husband's nephew."

"Then I suggest we prepare such a will at once!"

All three women smiled at Mr. Stockley and Lady Ratherby said, approvingly, "How right I was to choose you, sir. You have echoed our intentions precisely."

At that moment, a very tired Lord Pensley and Mr. Nicholson were headed south to Wallingford. With pressed lips Pensley wondered how thoroughly Cordelia would roast him for going off on this wild-goose chase or whether she would be so concerned for Drusilla that she would forbear to say anything at all.

As usual, Dr. Allenby took the back roads to

Ewelme. It was not a route he would have recommended to someone who did not know the way, but it was undeniably faster than going north to Shillingford and then east again. Besides, he had one or two calls to make on the way. He was quite pleased with himself as he drove with Mr. Julian Lawford beside him. Mrs. Lawford could not but be delighted to have her nephew so neatly delivered to her and she might, therefore, look with more kindness upon him when he proposed stealing her maid away from her. For although he had known Annie only a short time, Dr. Allenby was already certain that this was the woman he wished to marry.

23

Dr. Allenby was well-known at the Boarshead, and directly his tilbury drew to a halt in front of the inn, the ostler hurried forward to hold the reins for him. " 'Afternoon, Doctor.''

" 'Afternoon, Dixon. I don't know how long I shall be, as usual,'' he added with a smile.

"Don't you worrit none, I'll take good care of your horses, Doctor.''

"I know you will. Thank you,'' Allenby replied courteously before he led Julian inside. There he was also met with prompt attention, being a general favorite hereabouts. "Good afternoon, Severn. How is my patient today?''

The innkeeper, regarding Julian with interest, bowed toward both men as he replied, "In fine fettle, Doctor, what with her visitors and all.''

"Visitors?'' Julian asked sharply. "A gentleman perhaps? Or two?''

Severn shook his head. "No gentleman,'' he replied, having concluded that Mr. Stockley, the solicitor, ought not to be accorded such standing. "Mrs. Lawford's visitor was a lady, sir.''

"Oh, a lady.'' Julian shrugged, unable to conceive how a lady might be any danger to his plans. "Is she still here?''

Severn shook his head. "No, sir. The lady left a while ago to see our church of St. Mary the Virgin. Mrs. Lawford is in the private parlor, however, if you was wishing to see *her*."

"We are indeed." Dr. Allenby beamed. "I have brought her nephew with me today."

"Ah, that will please her." Severn nodded, eyes wide. "This way, not that you need me to be showing you, Doctor."

Nevertheless he did take them to the private parlor and rapped at the door. "Come in," a voice immediately called.

"Dr. Allenby, ma'am, and your nephew, or so I'm told."

It was impossible to tell who appeared more dismayed, Julian or Mrs. Lawford. "This is not my nephew," she said in thunderous accents. "I haven't any nephews."

"M-my apologies," Julian stammered. "I had thought you were someone else. The coincidence—"

Abruptly he stopped. The woman before him continued to stare fixedly at Julian and even Allenby quailed at her anger. Gradually dismay was replaced by a smile on Julian's face and he moved forward until he stood directly over her. With arms folded across his chest he said, "Very clever. I presume you are Mrs. Lawford's maid."

In outraged tones the woman replied, "How dare you, sir? It is the outside of enough for you to speak to me in such a way."

Even Allenby was moved to protest, "I say, Mr. Lawford, are you sure you haven't made a mistake?"

"Quite sure," Julian replied silkily. "You see, I recognize the dress this Mrs. Lawford is wearing."

"I will not answer such impertinence," Mrs. Lawford said with a distinct sniff.

"Where did you get the dress?" Julian went on inexorably. "You had not allowed for that, had you? But don't be afraid. I don't mean to cause you trouble. You may go when and where you wish, but not as Mrs. Lawford. I only want to know where she is to be found." The woman did not answer and he persisted, his voice still silky, "Come, tell me. Don't be afraid. Was she perhaps killed in an accident? And you decided to take her place? You need only tell me and write a statement to that effect and I shall leave you be."

Annie thought quickly. It was no use to deny who she was. This devil of a man would be so disloyal to his sex as to be able to remember Mrs. Lawford's dresses. The question was, could he be fobbed off with the tale that she was dead? And if so, would it be wise to put her name to such a statement?

In the end, however, it was Allenby who decided matters. "But if you were Mrs. Lawford's maid," he asked, utterly confused, "then who is *your* maid?"

Before Annie could concoct an answer, understanding lit Julian's eyes with an unholy gleam. "Clever," he hissed, "astonishingly clever. How unfortunate for you Dr. Allenby has taken such an interest in her. Who *is* she?" Annie pressed her lips together and Julian laughed triumphantly. "You exchanged places, didn't you? Very well, don't tell me. I shall find her anyway, I promise you."

And with that he turned and was gone. Trembling, Dr. Allenby asked Annie, "What is going on here?"

Bitterness filled her voice as she replied, "That man is Mrs. Lawford's nephew. He has already made one attempt to kill her by tampering with her carriage. After the accident she and I did, in fact, trade places. And now he has found us and I am helpless to go and warn her."

"Where is she? I'll take the message. Aye, and protect her, too, if I can," Allenby said curtly.

Annie did not hesitate, though she lowered her voice out of fear Julian might still be listening. "At the church. With Lady Ratherby. You must find her and tell her Julian is here."

"You may be sure I shall," he replied, then he too was gone.

Not twenty minutes later two more gentlemen stormed into her parlor. "Drusilla?" the first one called, not waiting to be announced.

"Lord Pensley!" Annie gasped.

Abruptly the two men halted. "Who the devil are you?" Pensley demanded.

"Her maid, Annie. And don't shout at me, m'lord. What I have to tell you is too important for that. She's in trouble. Julian Lawford is in Ewelme and knows she is here, dressed as a lady's maid. Dr. Allenby is trying to find her to warn her, but you'd best go after them right away. You'll find Mrs. Lawford with your sister at the church." She paused and added dryly, "You can't miss it, it's the tallest thing in town."

Pensley bowed. "My apologies. I shall go there straightaway. Come, Nicholson, we've no time to waste."

"Yes, yes, to be sure!"

Only when they were gone did Annie allow herself the luxury of a sigh of relief.

*   *   *

Julian saw Dr. Allenby enter the church of St.
Mary the Virgin just ahead of him. So the towns-
people had been right in saying she had gone in
there. Good. Let Dr. Allenby warn Drusilla. It would
make no difference in the end.

Once inside, it took a moment for Julian's eyes to
adjust to the change in lighting. Then he saw them, at
the far end of the church. Dr. Allenby was talking
animatedly to two women and a churchman. As he
watched, they turned and saw him. Immediately, one
of the women spoke to the churchman and he
hurried away into the back of the church. Dr. Allenby
came toward Lawford and the two women darted
into a side chapel. Julian had also been moving and
by now almost reached the midpoint of the church.

Allenby rushed forward and swung wildly at
Lawford.

Coolly Julian stepped aside and landed two blows,
and a moment later Allenby lay on the ground in-
sensible.

Without hesitating, Julian moved toward the
chapel the two ladies had entered. When he reached
it, he paused, taken aback by the sight of the
elaborate tomb that dominated the space and the
apparent absence of anyone there. Wildly he looked
about for an exit. When he saw none, he moved
forward gingerly, alert to any sound. And abruptly
he found them, crouched within a pew.

As he stared at the two women, they rose and
regarded him just as steadily. "Lady Ratherby,
Drusilla," he said silkily. "May I ask the reason for
this extraordinary exhibition?" Both ladies colored
and he went on, "You have no notion how foolish you
looked, crouched down like that. Or with dust all

over your skirts. Is this a new fashion, perhaps, playing at hide-and-quest? Are we to look for it at *ton* parties this spring? If so, I must beg to be excused, for children's games no longer amuse me, I fear."

"Please go away," Lady Ratherby said with what dignity she was able to muster.

Julian spread his hands. "But, my dear lady, I cannot. And it is not you I came to see, in any event. It is my dear Aunt Drusilla." Reproachfully he turned and looked at her. "Could you not have come to me when you felt this confusion overtaking you? This belief that you were a lady's maid?"

"I am not confused," Drusilla replied evenly, "nor do I think myself a servant. Annie and I have changed places because it seemed safer that way. Someone, perhaps upon your orders, tampered with our coach."

"Tampered with your coach?" Julian echoed, eyes opened wide. "But, my dearest aunt, that is impossible! Don't you recall that your own coachman looked it over carefully just before you left London? I thought that strange at the time, but surely you see that must refute your suspicions?"

"I own it was skillfully done," Drusilla replied, "but my coach was tampered with. Even the carriage smith in Wallingford agreed."

Sorrowfully Julian said, "That is not what he told me. Come, Aunt Drusilla, let us go home. You are most evidently under a strain and in need of rest. Let my mother and me take care of you. You cannot really think we mean you any harm."

Drusilla took a step backward. "No, Julian," she said decisively. "I shan't go anywhere with you. Particularly as Lady Ratherby has been so kind as to

tell me that all of London knows it was you who paid
Mrs. Crowley to spread doubt about my marriage to
Hugo."

Lawford darted a look of pure hatred at Cordelia.
"As Lord Pensley's sister can you dare to believe
her?" he asked derisively.

"Oh, I think so," Drusilla said calmly.

Julian sighed. "A pity, now we shall all of us have
to take a ride up to the hills in Dr. Allenby's tilbury.
It will no doubt be crowded, but we shall somehow
contrive."

Drusilla shook her head. "We won't go."

"I think you will," he answered evenly, drawing a
pistol from his coat pocket.

Lady Ratherby gasped. Drusilla, however, was
made of firmer stuff. "That won't work," she said.

"Oh, but it will," he replied. "We shall go up into
the hills and there will be an accident and both of
you will be killed. I shall be slightly injured and
desolate."

"And you will inherit my estate?" Drusilla said
mildly.

"So you remember that," Julian observed. "How
clever of you."

"More clever than you realize," Cordelia put in.

That was a mistake. The pistol now veered toward
her. "What Lady Ratherby means," Drusilla said
calmly, "is that you inherit only if I die intestate, and
I have just this morning drawn up my will, leaving
everything to various charities."

"You are lying," he snarled. "Trying to bluff your
way free."

Drusilla shook her head. "Unfortunately for you, I
am not. Lady Ratherby brought with her from
Wallingford a solicitor and he is no on his way back

there with one copy of the will. A second copy is here, in the care of the vicar of Ewelme. I thought, you see, that you might wish to consult it, if you came," she added ironically.

"If what you say is true, why should I not simply shoot you for all the trouble you have caused me?" Julian demanded.

"Because if you do, I shall see you hung," Lord Pensley's voice rang out behind them.

Startled, the three turned to see Pensley holding his own pistol trained upon Julian, Nicholson by his side. "Not only should I see you hung," his lordship went on conversationally, "but I should shoot you in the leg just to make sure you could not run away."

Julian lowered his own pistol and then dropped it to the floor. "It seems you have the advantage of me," he said finally. "What am I to do now? Flee to the Continent? I haven't any funds to do so, but perhaps you would be prepared to pay to have me out of the way?"

"No," Pensley replied, "I expect you are still going to hang for murder."

"*What?*" the three in the chapel demanded in unison.

"The fellow in the church, Dr. Allenby, I presume, is badly hurt and I fear he may well die," Pensley said grimly. "He appears to have struck his head against a stone pillar and the vicar tells me it was your fault, Lawford."

Julian dived for the pistol he had dropped and Pensley fired his own. Clutching his arm, Lawford fell to the floor and Nicholson hastily ran forward to grab the gun. "I told you I was an excellent shot," his lordship said coolly. "Now up on your feet, we'll need to find the nearest magistrate."

"I can't! I need a doctor!" Julian whimpered, his face contorted with pain.

Looking down at Lawford, Pensley said impassively, "What a pity, then, that you may have killed the only one in Ewelme."

24

"But he can't truly hang for that," Drusilla protested. "It was an accident!"

Even Lady Ratherby said quietly, "I own I should like to see him hung, but Drusilla is right."

"Well, the wait in jail will do him good," Nicholson said, quivering with distress. "In all my years as a solicitor I have never seen such monstrous behavior."

Looking down at Drusilla, Lord Pensley smiled wryly and said, "You are all of you quite right, but I had hoped to at least put a scare into Julian Lawford."

"And so you have," a voice snarled from the floor. With an effort that was visible to everyone there, Lawford pulled himself up to his feet. Swaying slightly, he said, "Do you think I care whether I hang? When the alternative is to be reduced to penury and when I know every member of the *ton* will turn their back upon me after this? It is Hugo's fault, you know. If he hadn't been such a heartless, selfish fellow I should never have found myself in such a desperate fix. He refused to bail me out when he was alive and even in death he contrived at my ruin. Leaving a fortune to *her!* Pah. She would have done well enough with a small competence. She hasn't the imagination, as I do, to know what can be done with such a fortune."

"You mean start up the Hell-Fire Club again?" Pensley asked quietly.

Julian fixed a wavering stare upon his lordship. "Oh, sneer if you like. But no, the members of the *ton* I know are all too fainthearted for such a scheme." With an evil grin he said, "I shan't tell you what I planned, but you may believe it would have made the Hell-Fire Club seem quite innocuous. Only you've put paid to those plans, haven't you? All of you, acting together. Very well, then I've nothing to lose."

Before anyone could react, Julian Lawford had thrown himself forward and reached for the pistol Nicholson still held. They struggled and just as Pensley grabbed Julian to pull him off, a shot rang out.

For a moment no one knew what had happened as both men fell to the floor senseless. Immediately Cordelia and Drusilla were down beside them, one grabbing for the pistol, the other feeling for a pulse. "Mr. Nicholson is alive," Cordelia all but shouted with relief.

"And Julian Lawford?" Pensley demanded.

"Dead," was his sister's brief reply.

Quietly Drusilla got to her feet and handed the pistol to Lord Pensley. "Here, I think you'd better take charge of this," she said.

He nodded. From behind them the vicar of Ewelme came forward, scandalized. "Gunshots. I heard gunshots. In my church!"

His emotions rigidly held in check, Lord Pensley turned to explain to the vicar precisely what had occurred.

*   *   *

It was two mornings later when Lord Pensley, who had since moved his sister and himself to Ewelme, entered the private parlor of the Boarshead and advanced upon Drusilla, who stood by the window. She was once more dressed in her proper clothing and around her shoulders was the length of Indian muslin Cordelia had persuaded her to buy in London. Annie, whose ankle had finally healed, was upstairs preparing for their return to London. "H-hello, Lord Pensley," Drusilla said warily.

Richard now stood over her, and biting off each word, he said, "If you ever give me such a fright again, my love, I shall . . ." But before he could complete his threat, he pulled Drusilla to him, his arms encircling her in a crushing grip. Hungrily he kissed her. "I was so afraid Julian would kill you," Richard managed at last to say.

Drusilla rested her head against his shoulder as she replied, "So was I. We have a great deal to thank your sister for. And Nicholson. How is he?"

"As well as can be expected. Physically he has completely recovered from the shock, which was his only injury. But I gather his nerves are still overset. He chose to return to London yesterday, stopping by way of Mr. Stockley's office in Wallingford. He meant to take a copy of your will to London with him and call upon Elizabeth Lawford. Someone must tell her what happened to Julian and see what her wishes are as to his burial. He will also see to it that she knows she cannot benefit by your death," Richard replied.

"She is more likely to be concerned about vengeance, I should think," Drusilla observed with a sigh.

"Nicholson will also make it clear to her what will

happen if she tries." He paused and then added, "We, both of us, blame ourselves that we did not think to have you write a will sooner. Before I sent you out of London. Can you forgive me for that?"

Drusilla looked up at Richard steadily. "There is nothing to forgive. Had I thought about it, I too should have recollected that damnable provision. But even if I had, or you had, I should have found it impossible to believe such a step was necessary. How could I? Julian was all that was kind to me, and while I might believe he was behind the attempts to discredit me, how could I have thought he would try murder? Even now it seems fantastic." She paused, then with an effort smiled. "Come," she rallied him, "tell me about Cordelia."

With an attempt to lighten her mood Richard said, "We are in for it, I fear. Cordelia has been telling me that we are commanded to visit Ratherby's estate and tell his children all about her adventure, for otherwise she is convinced they will never believe their mother to be a heroine."

"How true." Drusilla laughed in sympathy. "When are we to go there?"

"Upon our honeymoon, she tells me," Pensley retorted dryly.

"Our honeymoon?" Drusilla asked innocently, pressing her face against his shoulder where he could not see her dancing eyes.

"My dear Mrs. Lawford," he said in wounded accents, "did you think I was merely trifling with you? That I treated every pretty widow this way? No, no, no, you are to marry me so that I may have your wealth within my clutches."

In a small voice she said, "I had not thought it

possible you were a heartless libertine, but then you have not mentioned marriage until just now."

"I told you at Vauxhall Gardens I meant to marry you," Pensley reminded Drusilla. "But these past two days I have had other matters on my mind, such as Julian's death and Dr. Allenby's tenuous recovery."

Drusilla pulled free. "It all seems very cruel," she said, no longer bantering.

"That was another reason I did not speak of marriage these past two days," Richard replied. "I knew you would be overset by what happened."

"Poor Elizabeth, I cannot help but feel for her," Drusilla told Pensley. "Even though I know you have said she had a part in this as well." Drusilla paused. "Will you tell me why you hated Julian so much? Aside from his attempt upon my life and nearly killing Dr. Allenby, for that was an accident."

"I doubt he would agree," Pensley said dryly. "Julian Lawford meant to ensure that Allenby could not stop his plans, and he cared very little how badly hurt the doctor might be." Pensley stopped and seemed to debate with himself before he went on. "Have you seen him yet today?"

"Yes. And Dr. Jenkins, the man they brought in from Wallingford, says that he will be on his feet in a few days." She paused and smiled. "Dr. Allenby is as impatient for that as anyone could be. He keeps talking of all the patients he must see."

"Yes, I have been made aware that Allenby is a popular figure hereabouts, and I cannot doubt the reason why," Richard replied. "Was he angry over your masquerade?"

Drusilla shook her head. "No, he understood very

well that my life was at stake. He said that after his encounter with Julian he could not doubt it. Indeed, Dr. Allenby was quite the gentleman, saying that while he might aspire to the hand of a lady's maid, he knew he must relinquish the field to you now that I stand revealed as who I am."

"You liked him, didn't you?" Richard asked.

"Yes, I did," Drusilla said frankly. "He was kind and intelligent and very likable. But I find there is someone I care for more." Pensley smiled at her warmly and she said a trifle severely, "We have talked about Dr. Allenby long enough, however. You were to tell me why you disliked Julian so deeply."

Pensley sighed. "Very well. I have always disliked Julian Lawford. I know of more than one young girl he left pregnant and then deserted. Servants, usually, who then found themselves dismissed from their work and homeless as well. There are rumors he once held up a stagecoach with friends for a lark. Unfortunately, the coachman was killed, but nothing was ever proved against Julian and his friends. These are the things I knew of Julian when I warned you against him back in London, but I am afraid there is much worse. Hugo left a letter with his chief wallah. In it he gave his reasons for marrying you and he stated that Julian Lawford had attempted to revive the Hell-Fire Club. You may not know of it, but I assure you the name was well suited. I have since made inquiries and discovered that the attempt failed only because there were a few unfortunate deaths, none of which could be proved but which scared off prospective members. I hold Julian Lawford responsible for those deaths."

Drusilla was silent for several moments. At last she said, "Yes, I see. I shan't mourn for him then; he needed to be stopped." She paused, then added wanly, "So Hugo left a letter? Well, at least the *ton* must accept me as Hugo's widow, then. I suppose I have you to thank for that."

Pensley once more pulled Drusilla tightly into his arms. "Nicholson. He is the one who sent someone to India to discover the truth of your story more than a year ago. As for me, I should rather," he said, "that you were concerned the *ton* accept you as Lady Pensley. And I should like to send the announcement to the *Gazette* as soon as we have returned to London. So will you marry me, my beloved?"

When she could catch her breath sufficiently to answer, sometime later Drusilla replied, her eyes dancing, "I suppose I must, m'lord. Now that I have sunk myself beneath reproach by behaving this way with you I must do *something* to retrieve my shocking reputation."

Before she could say anything more, Pensley swept Drusilla up into a tight embrace again. And she met his kisses more eagerly than ever.

About the Author

April Lynn Kihlstrom was born in Buffalo, New York, and graduated from Cornell University with an M.S. in Operations Research. She, her husband, and their two children enjoy traveling and have lived in Paris, Honolulu, Georgia, and New Jersey. When not writing, April Lynn Kihlstrom enjoys needlework and devotes her time to handicapped children.

Her lips were still warm from the imprint of his kiss, but now Silvia knew there was nothing to protect her from the terror of Serpent Tree Hall. Not even love. Especially not love. . . .

DARK SPLENDOR

ANDREA PARNELL

Lovely young Silvia Bradstreet had come from London to Colonial America to be a bondservant on an isolated island estate off the Georgia coast. But a far different fate awaited her at the castle-like manor: a man whose lips moved like a hot flame over her flesh . . . whose relentless passion and incredible strength aroused feelings she could not control. And as a whirlpool of intrigue and violence sucked her into the depths of evil . . . flames of desire melted all her power to resist. . . .

Coming in September from Signet!